I0533789

DOUBLE ACTING

JESS MOWRY

Copyright © 2015 - 2020 by Jess Mowry

PRINT ISBN-10: 0-9985579-1-9
PRINT ISBN-13: 978-0-9985579-1-5

EBOOK ISBN-10: 0-9977994-5-5
EBOOK ISBN-13: 978-0-9977994-5-3

First Anubis Edition 2017

OTHER BOOKS BY JESS MOWRY

Rats In The Trees
Children Of The Night
Way Past Cool
Six Out Seven
Ghost Train
Babylon Boyz
Phat Acceptance
Voodoo Dawgz
Bones Become Flowers
Tyger Tales
When All Goes Bright
Skeleton Key
Knights Crossing
The Bridge
Reaps
Magic Rats
Midnight Sons
Drawing From Life
The Coyote Valley Railroad
In The Dead Of Night
Ghost Ship
Spencer's Spirit
The Insiders
The Light

TO BERT WALKER

DOUBLE ACTING

"That's the last of it, dad," panted Mike, trudging out of the small shabby house.

It was only a little past noon, but the day was already blazing hot, and Mike was shirtless in jeans and sneaks, his muscular body shiny with sweat. He was only thirteen, but his chest was a pair of high-jutting bricks, his belly a perfectly sculpted six-pack, while his biceps bulged like baseballs even though relaxed. He was black as a panther at midnight, with a gently-rounded snub-nosed face, full expressive pouty lips usually showing big white teeth, and large and long-lashed ebony eyes. He wore his hair in a bushy mop beneath a battered newsboy cap, a relic he'd found in a pawn shop, which gave a him a *Little Rascals* look like sort of an older and super-buff Buckwheat.

His father was closing the doors of the rented cargo trailer. The man was almost as dark as Mike, thirty-seven and strongly built though a little rolly around the waist (he laughed at Mike's gentle urgings to jog) and also clad in jeans and sneaks. "Welcome to Coyote Valley,

1

son. We should have a beer to celebrate, but there's nothing except bottled water."

"And that's not even cold," puffed Mike, wiping sweat off his face. "When will they turn on the power?"

His father glanced at a sun-weathered pole out by the road that ran past the house. "They should have done it already. I sent an email a week ago, but people move slower out here."

"I can see why!" Mike doffed his cap for a moment and dog-shook sweat from his hair. "I never knew it could get this hot, even with climate change."

"It got this hot when I was your age and spent a summer here with my uncle."

"Wasn't that kinda boring?" asked Mike. "Since you were raised in Oakland?"

"It was at first," said his dad. "But it kept me out of city trouble... gangs, drugs, violence, etcetera... and at just the right time in my life when I'd started thinking 'bad' might be cool. But wait until August if you think it's hot now, this is just early June. ...Think you can handle this, son?"

Mike puffed his chest, though it didn't need puffing. "I'm in good shape so I can take it. Don't worry about me, just finish your book, it's gonna be a best-seller this time."

His father looked thoughtful. "Wish I could be that sure. Every black book is a *first* book no matter how many you've sold before. ...And don't push yourself too hard with those weights. You're only thirteen once in this life, so just kick back and enjoy it sometimes. Don't always feel compelled to *do* something, or guilty for just day-dreaming a while. 'Getting active' includes your mind, and dreams are healthy, too. They get us in shape for our future. You might not understand that now, but trust me you will when you're my age and remember what you *didn't* enjoy when you had the chance."

"Like, 'take time to smell the flowers?'" Mike glanced around. "If there were any flowers out here."

"There may not be any flowers *per se*, but the desert has its own kind of beauty and I enjoyed my summer here. Did a lot of reading and dreaming in the shade of that water tank out back."

Mike laughed. "Which might be why you became a writer. ...But weren't you worried about getting fat?"

"Kids didn't obsess about weight in those days because we weren't bullied, bullshitted and brainwashed to believe that being chubby or fat meant we were lazy, ugly and stupid and/or a threat to society. But I did a lot of exploring, too." Mike's father pointed north-east. "There's a big copper mine three miles up the road... though Uncle Joe wrote it closed last year, about six months before he passed. He also told me stories about a ghost town up in those mountains. I always wanted to check it out, but that would have been a three day trip... a thirty mile hike up an old railroad track." He laughed. "And I didn't want to spend a night alone in an old ghost town."

"'Cause of ghosts?" asked Mike.

"To be honest, yes. But now I wish I had."

"Would you like to go back and be thirteen again? Do some of the stuff you didn't do?"

"It's the time to go exploring, physically and mentally. Some would also say spiritually, like Indian boys on vision quests."

"What if I got obese 'cause I did too much mental exploring? And I don't guess the spiritual kind burns any calories either."

The man patted Mike's stone-hard belly. "There would be more of you to love, not that there isn't plenty already." He poked one of Mike's jutting pecs with a finger. "Clichéd as it probably sounds, it's what's inside a person that counts. And some of the so-called 'healthiest' bodies have the sickest little minds." He latched the trailer's doors. "I have get this into town or they'll charge for another day. Want to come along?"

Mike had already seen the "town," appropriately named Coyote Flats, when they'd driven though on their way out here; a sun-baked huddle of ramshackle buildings, most of wood with archaic false fronts, that looked like an old western movie set. Maybe because of the hellish heat there hadn't been many people outdoors; and, brown, white, or copper-toned (he'd assumed the latter were In-dians) none had looked very Active. The only kids in evidence, three shirtless boys in dusty jeans, who might have been around ten or eleven and represented all three colors, were sitting in front of the small general

3

store leisurely licking ice cream cones; one boy chubby, another fat, and the third undisputedly obese. "Nah, that's cool. I'll start unpacking and set up my weights."

"Going to set up your train, too?"

"...I don't know," said Mike. "Maybe I should have sold it to help us pay for gas."

"We're not that poor," said his dad. "And you spent lots of time building that layout."

"Not to mention money."

"Money is to use, Mike, not only for things you need, but also for things that make you happy. We had some then, and we'll have some again. And it's still my job to worry about it."

"I was pretty out of shape just working on my train all the time."

His father gave Mike a hug. "You're always in perfect shape to me." He got into the battered Land Rover, a 1963 Series Two. "Just take it easy at first. You're not used to this Arizona heat. Drink lots of water, even if you're not feeling thirsty."

Mike patted his chest. "I wouldn't wanna get dehydrated, you lose muscle mass that way."

"Okay, Mr. Teenage Universe." His father glanced at a rusty windmill on a skeletal tower behind the house. The tower was maybe forty feet tall, and at its base on timber legs was a weathered wooden water tank. "Speaking of water... and if you want to 'get active'... climb up there and unlock the vane. It's chained so the fins can't turn."

"Why is it chained?" asked Mike.

"You chain it when the wind gets too strong, otherwise it could be damaged by turning too fast."

"But there's no wind."

"There's strong winds here in the spring and fall. Uncle Joe passed in February and someone, maybe a neighbor, chained the windmill down. But there's usually an evening breeze, so it can start pumping tonight. The tank is probably empty and the planks have shrunk, so it's going to leak for a while. Best get it started filling now if you want to take a shower next week."

"Okay," said Mike, eyeing the tower. "That'll be good exercise... but I'm really gonna smell in a week."

"You've never offended my nose; and desert people tend to smell earthy. But I'll buy a couple of water cans to get us through until the tank fills. ...And, speaking of mass, what do you want for dinner?"

"I saw a KFC in town... at least the sign on a shack."

"Regular or grilled?"

"What's the point of grilled if it's supposed to be KFC? ...I'm not a *health-nazi*, dad!"

His father laughed. "Those people are *really* out of shape in all the ways that matter. ...I should be back in a couple of hours. Stay out of trouble, muscle-boy."

Mike gazed around at the desolate landscape of shimmering rust-colored desert. It reminded him of pictures of Mars. It was totally flat except for mountains, jagged and barren in the distance, that seemed to rise from rocky rubble. Otherwise there was nothing but sagebrush, and cactus bristling with savage spikes. "To get into trouble there's gotta be some, and I don't think there's any for a hundred miles."

His dad started the Land Rover's engine, which rattled a bit in the heat. "There's lots of rattlesnakes around here, and they can be trouble if you don't respect them."

Mike looked around again. "I haven't seen any."

"But I'm sure they've seen you. I left the snake-bite kit on the table. Check it out and read the instructions. Snakes won't bother you if you don't bother them, but be careful when you're walking around... look before you step over a rock to see what's on the other side. And don't reach into dark places."

Mike smiled. "Thanks for all the healthy advice."

5

TWO

The road was only a twin-rutted trail, and the Rover raised a long tail of dust as it rocked and rattled away with the empty trailer booming behind. The sound of its engine faded, leaving only sweltering silence. Mike watched from the shade of the house's front porch until the vehicle reached the junction where the trail met a ribbon of two-lane highway, deserted except for a lone semi-truck which was only a speck in the distance. The junction was maybe a mile away, and there was a little general store that looked like an old trading-post in a movie -- except for a pair of pumps in front, one for gas and the other for diesel -- its faded false-front sign reading

GRISWOLD'S

GENERAL

MERCHANDISE

They had stopped to buy Cokes coming in, Mike gratefully gulping a 16 ounce (and trying not to feel guilty about it) and the air-conditioning had felt like heaven after driving all night in the dry desert heat.

He scanned around again: there were only two other buildings in sight. To the south, about halfway to the store, was a small ancient house of unpainted wood. Behind it was a big water tank like those in the days of steam locomotives; and there was a rusty windmill tower, its blades hanging motionless in the breathless air. In the house's front yard was an old yellow dump truck. Mike had been dozing when they'd driven past, but now he squinted at the truck. There was something wrong with the perspective; the truck looked almost as big as the house! Maybe it was closer and not really parked in front?

To the north, up the road, was a big mobile home, a double-wide that looked fairly new, its white paint gleaming painfully. It was maybe a quarter mile away, and there was a swimming pool in front; one of those above-ground kind. Mike imagined how good it would feel to be in that sparkling water. He wondered if any kids lived there... hopefully around his own age. Then he opened the squeaky screen door.

His new home was a tumbledown shack of sun-blasted boards with four little rooms and a rusty tin roof. There was some junky furniture in what passed for a living room... a sagging couch, an over-stuffed chair that was no longer "over," a homemade wooden coffee table, and all of it furry with rust-colored dust. A kerosene lantern hung from a rafter beside a naked light bulb as if both were of equal importance. The floor was bare boards, also covered with dust, and moving boxes were scattered around, though Mike and his dad hadn't brought very much because they didn't have very much... thanks to Mike's mother, who'd won a big chunk of his dad's book earnings, still claiming -- despite her live-in boyfriend and a nice bungalow in Culver City -- she needed financial support.

There was a telephone on a wall, black like all phones used to be. Mike's grandmother -- his mother's mother -- had often sadly shaken her head and called Mike "black as a telephone." Mike's mother, much lighter than his dad, had always seemed concerned by his color, remarking he "didn't come out" in photos and trying to make him wear a shirt whenever he was in the sun (which, of course, he'd always lost as soon as he was out of her sight). And once, when he'd been eleven, he'd overheard her telling his dad that, if they'd only had more money "Mike could have his complexion lightened," which had given him a nightmare of being transformed into Michael Jackson.

But money, or rather the lack of it in a steady stream from a "real job," had always been her main complaint until she'd left three years ago.

The phone had buttons instead of a dial but still looked a hundred years old. Mike lifted the dusty receiver but didn't hear a tone. He jiggled the hook but still got nothing. The swamp-cooler wouldn't work either until there was electricity, so it was hotter in here than outside.

On another wall hung a framed photograph, a old black-and-white faded to sepia, of a little steam train on a narrow-gauge track, and Mike brushed some of the dust off the glass. His own model layout was steam, with an Eclipse 0-6-0 locomotive... which looked like the one in this picture. The setting was in a desert, and he wondered if this was the train that had run to the ghost town over the mountains. Looking closer, he made out the words

COYOTE VALLEY RAILROAD

on the locomotive's tender, which seemed to confirm it was... or had been. The date in a corner of the photo was June 13, 1897.

He went into his own little room, which also contained a few moving boxes, including one full of books. Mike read a lot, though these days mostly in bed at night because it wasn't an Active pastime. Another box held his H.O. train, though there hadn't been space in the trailer to bring the layout board. He would have to build another layout... assuming he wanted to.

They hadn't brought any furniture, selling it all to help pay for gas, and Mike's "new" bed was an iron skeleton with a starving mattress on rusty springs. There was a dynamite box beside it front-ing as a night table, with a kerosene lantern on top, plus a shabby chest of drawers with a darkly de-silvering mirror. A bare bulb hung on frayed wires from a rafter, and his weight bench stood half set up in a corner. He would have to find something to use as a desk to put his computer and games on. He was good with tools, thanks to helping his dad with projects on their former home, so he could build a book shelf.

The room was like a pizza oven set for extra-crispy crust. Mike's jeans were soaked and heavy with sweat from toting in the boxes, and his shorts felt like he'd gone swimming in them. He stripped buck-bare except for his cap, then opened the one grimy window -- its frame, like all the wood in the house, shriveled by decades of desert heat -- which only seemed to increase the heat. He glanced at the other old house in the distance -- the truck couldn't be *that* big! -- then studied himself in the murky mirror. His body looked cool all shiny with sweat, like he'd oiled for a muscle-building show -- not that he'd ever been in one, except when posing for himself, which he proceeded to do, flexing his biceps and puffing his pecs -- but damn it was hot! Maybe he should start unpacking and finish setting up his weights?

But it was too hot for that now. He thought about sweeping the dust from his room -- it was like an indoor desert -- but it was too hot to do anything! He padded into the tiny kitchen at the back of the house, which boasted a box-like wood-burning stove and a tin sink with only one faucet. The rusty refrigerator, a 1930s General Electric with motor and cooling coils on top, wasn't working, of course, but he drank a hot bottle of water, one of four left in a six-pack. That reminded him of the windmill.

He opened the back door and studied the tower. There was an iron ladder, so climbing would be no problem. Would he need tools? His dad's toolbox was in the Rover, but he had a small set of his own. He should take a couple of Crescent wrenches in case the chain was bolted.

The tower wasn't far away, maybe a hundred feet, and the ground was open except for sagebrush, and cactus bristling with attitude... nowhere, it seemed, for a snake to hide. He noticed a half-collapsed outhouse, which obviously hadn't been used since indoor plumbing had been installed... maybe fifty years ago. A snake might be lurking inside. Would it come after him?

He took the snake-bite kit off the kitchen table. The instructions were in pictures, and he winced at the one that showed how to slice. ...But, what if he got bit on his butt? He felt around on his tight behind and decided he could manage. He took the kit into his room, donned a fresh pair of jeans commando -- it was too hot for boxers -- put on his sneaks without socks, and slipped the kit into a pocket. Then he got the wrenches and went out through the kitchen door.

Total silence ruled the desert. Total silence and hellish heat.

Staying away from the outhouse in case it did conceal a serpent, he went to the tower and mounted the ladder. Climbing was harder than he'd expected; despite being in healthy shape, the heat seemed to suck out his strength, and he was panting and pouring sweat by the time he'd climbed the first twenty feet. His jeans were sodden and slipping low, and he paused at the top of the water tank to pull them up his hips. The tank had a wooden cover, and there was a little trap door. He opened the door and peered in. Like his father had said, it was empty, and there were slits of sunlight where its planks had shrunk. "Boo!" he called like a little kid, and got a spooky echo.

Closing the door, he continued his climb, and after a lot more panting and sweating, finally reached the top of the tower, which gave him a lofty bird's-eye view of the sun-shimmered valley floor. To the west was basically nothing until the mountains rose. To the north-east was a gigantic hole that looked like a meteor crater, but was probably the copper mine. Maybe twenty miles to the south were the clustered buildings of Coyote Flats. To the east was also basically nothing to the rubble-strewn feet of those mountains.

Then he noticed a narrow line that might have been a railroad track. It was almost buried by sagebrush and cactus, but angled south-west from the copper mine to run past the big water tank behind the house down the road... which must have been a water stop for steam trains long ago.

Then he examined the windmill. The chain had been knotted, not bolted, and it only took a minute to untie the links and extend the vane. He figured out how to latch it in place -- steam-age tech-nology -- then rotated the rusty fins. The bearings should have been oiled, but the oil can was in the Rover, so he'd do that when his dad returned. Then he climbed wearily down. Reaching the ground and dripping more sweat, he looked back up the tower. It couldn't be more than forty feet tall, but he felt like he'd climbed four-hundred!

He thought of ice-cold drinks at the store. It was only a mile away.

THREE

The afternoon was even hotter as Mike came out on the house's front porch clad in fresh jeans and sneaks without socks. Sweat trickled down from under his arms, the scent of him strong in the sweltering air but basically boyish and not really bad. Healthy sweat, he supposed.

His BMX leaned against the porch rail, but he paused to consider if it was smart to try to ride anywhere in this heat. A shadow swept over the ground as a real Hollywood movie vulture came to rest on the telephone pole and seemed to eye him in speculation as if he might make a healthy meal. Would it follow him if he rode to the store?

Looking away uneasily, he scanned the heat-shimmered landscape. The sky was cloudless and brilliantly blue, and the line of telephone poles by the road dwindled into infinity like a drawing lesson in vanishing-points. He shaded his eyes from the glare of sunlight blazing on basically nothing. South was the highway, and there was the store. Closer stood the ancient house with its strangely huge truck in front... it couldn't be *that* big! Up the rutted road to the north was the mobile home with its swimming pool... which looked like an oasis.

He imagined a beautiful girl lived there. A girl of thirteen, of course. She would go swimming every day in nothing but a bikini. ...Maybe, since there was no one around, she would go swimming without the bikini! She probably wouldn't be black, but Mike wasn't prejudiced... assuming she wasn't. His dad had a pair of binoculars, so Mike could peep her on the sly... maybe from the windmill tower. Her breasts would be large and perfectly round, and she would have a Hollywood body with everything else that promised. He pictured

11

himself going swimming with her, and maybe doing... other things. Like hugging and kissing at least. She would be smart, but not *too* smart. At least no smarter than him.

Mike had imagined her so well that he forgot he was. How to make first contact? Why not ride his bike up the road? The girl would be getting ready to swim, putting on her bikini right now... or maybe putting on nothing. She would be lonely all by herself way out here in the desert. The timing would be perfect! She would come out as he rode by. And he would be all sweaty, so she would offer him something to drink. Maybe even an ice-cold beer.

He started to mount his bike despite the ominous vulture... but then someone *did* come out on the porch of the distant mobile home!

Mike felt a little shocked... like he'd wished for something and gotten it, but wasn't sure what to do with it. He'd always been shy around girls, but, by building up his body, he'd found them to be more attracted to him. Not that it had gotten him much: the ones who wanted to feel his muscles and always begged him to lose his shirt never had anything to say... at least not much he wanted to hear. And they only read books when they had to for school. He shaded his eyes with a hand and frowned... it wasn't a girl, dammit!

It was hard to see in the distance through shimmering ghosts of heat, but it seemed to be a young boy; a gawky and sloppily swag-bellied boy clad in nothing but short cut-off jeans. Maybe he was going swimming? The kid descended the porch's steps, but mounted a red minibike, the kind with small wheels and a skeleton frame. He reached down and pulled the starter rope. There was a burst of blue-tinted smoke, and a moment later came the snarl of a bratty one-cylinder engine. The kid throttled up and burned away, skidding sideways into the road and roaring in Mike's direction while trailing a streamer of dust. The vulture gave a croak and took off.

Was the kid on his way to the store, Mike wondered? Or was he coming to check his new neighbors? Mike decided to be cool: like his father had said, you never got a second-chance to make a first-impression.

Pretending he hadn't noticed the kid, he leaned his bike against the porch rail and walked to the mailbox out by the road as if just going to check it. He waited until the minibike had gotten close before turning to look, though only a deaf person wouldn't have heard it miles away in the sultry silence. The boy locked the brake and slid to stop, spewing dust all over Mike.

The boy looked about twelve with a mop of blond hair that smothered his narrow shoulders and almost covered big blue eyes, and had what Mike called a "gamer body," shapelessly soft and slackly rolly with bobby boy-breasts for a chest... sort of how Mike had looked last year. But this kid had an appalling belly besides just being out of shape; a wobbly mass like a pillow of pudding that spilled onto the bike's gas tank like some sort of sloppy saddlebag, its navel like a smart-ass smirk. He was deeply tanned to an old-penny shade, which made his blue eyes even brighter and his shaggy hair look almost white. He had a puggy-nosed impish face with a hint of a small second chin, and huge buck teeth that he didn't brush much and might have opened bottlecaps. Except for being so out of shape, and not packing a boomerang, he reminded Mike of the feral kid in the *Road Warrior* movie.

He wore a punk necklace of chrome steel beads that looked like an oversize bathtub chain, and a massive Rolex on one wrist... stainless steel with multiple dials that looked like it needed a license to own and a training course to operate. On his other wrist were some colored cloth bands, though Mike had never learned the code. Around one ankle was another steel chain, and low on his hips was a wide leather belt and an old cowboy gun in a holster, so massive it looked like a cartoon cannon, its barrel almost dragging the ground. Most of the bluing was worn off its steel, leaving it dull silver-gray, and its brass parts were tarnished dark gold. Mike didn't know much about guns, but he'd seen hundreds in pawn shops when his father's royalty checks had dwindled, and this might have been an old Navy Colt.

"Wuttup, nigga?" the kid greeted Mike, over the chug of his idling engine.

Mike was shocked, then felt pissed. "What did you call me?"

"I said it with an A," said the kid, sounding innocent enough despite being heavily armed. "Don't you call yourselfs niggas?"

"Only retarded niggas."

13

The kid smirked. "Or maybe only retarded ones don't."

Mike decided to stay cool and pretended to check the mailbox, which had a huge spider inside. It was only a little kid... even if he had a gun.

"It *came* already," said the kid. "It *cuuums* in the mornin'," he added, as if Mike hadn't gotten the clue. "Expectin' a *Hustler?*"

"No!" said Mike, slamming the box.

"I gots a subscription," announced the kid, which pretty much trashed his innocence. "What's your name? I'm Carson."

"Mike," said Mike.

"I mean your street name."

"Mike," said Mike.

"You smoke, homeboy?"

"Hell no! It's the worst thing you can do to yourself, except for getting obese."

"Bullshit," said the kid. "I smoked since I was eight." He patted his wobbly sprawl of belly, which quivered to the throb of the engine as if it was its own life form. "An' I'm healthier than you are, homes."

"Like shit!" said Mike, puffing his chest. Except for his dramatic tan, the kid looked exactly like a gamer who sprawled on a couch or his bed all day, never ate anything but junk, or used any muscles except in his fingers.

"Yeah?" said Carson. "I ain't the one all sweaty an' pantin' like a dog."

Mike scowled for a moment. Carson stank of tobacco smoke, and there was beer on his breath. And there was another suggestive scent that proved he wasn't innocent... at least not with himself. Mike decided the kid was drunk so maybe he should cut him some slack... and he had said it with an A. "I'm just not used to this heat."

Carson blasted a burp, strongly scenting the air with beer. "Ain't it hot in Africa?"

"...Not so much in California."

"Cool! Hollywood?"

"Thousand Oaks."

"Is there?" asked Carson.

"Is there what?"

14

Carson snickered. "A thousand oaks, duh. Did you count 'em to make sure you wasn't cheated?"

"That's retarded."

"You're retarded." Carson checked Mike up and down. "How'd you get all them muscles?"

"I work out and eat healthy."

"That's gotta be a borin' life. You drink beer at least?"

"Sometimes."

"Maybe there's hope for you yet, my man. Gots any?"

Mike was starting to get really pissed... but the kid had a swimming pool. "My dad will probably bring some back: he went to drop off the trailer in town."

"Does he smoke?"

"Hell no!"

"What's his game?"

"What do you mean?"

"You sure you're black? What's he do for green, duh?"

"He writes books."

"Dirty books?"

"No, goddammit! Ghost stories."

"That's kinda cool," Carson conceded. "Are they full of blood an' guts, an' people gettin' their faces ripped off?"

"They're the classical kind, with haunted houses... like, set in Victorian times."

"Like steam punk with ghosts?"

"...Guess you could say that," said Mike.

"I mostly watch movies," said Carson. "Only read when they make me in school."

"Big surprise," said Mike.

"We gots a dish. Gets 200 channels. You gonna get one, bra?"

"...Maybe."

"Ya better, dawg. 'Cause otherwise there's only two channels an' both of 'em suck like ten-dollar ho's. Does your dad make lots of money?"

Mike shrugged. "Enough... most of the time. But writing's not a steady income." He thought of his mom always grabbing a chunk --

15

though she'd finally made a settlement by taking the house in Thousand Oaks, since his father's writing career "would never amount to anything" -- but that was nobody's business. Especially a drunk little kid's. "That's why we came out here," he added. "My great-uncle left him this house. ...Did you know him?"

"Yeah, he was cool," said Carson... which surprised Mike a little. "Told me stories about this place when it was back in the gold minin' days." He pointed north-east. "Said when he first come here... like, maybe when he was your age... there was a train went over them mountains to a town called Codyville. 'Cept it's a ghost town today. You can still see the tracks goin' up to the pass." Then he smirked again. "But now it's mostly losers who end up in Coyote Valley."

"You're in Coyote Valley," said Mike.

"I was born here, what's your excuse? My mom's a cocktail waitress at the Rattlesnake Saloon in town. *That's* a steady income, doc. She gets lots of tips an' buys me stuff."

"That's nice," said Mike. He wondered if he should blow the kid off... but he had a swimming pool.

"What kinda ride you roll?" asked Carson.

"My dad has a Land Rover."

"Like a Jeep?"

"Way better," said Mike.

"How much it cost?"

"It's an old one, a classic. Like in African movies."

"Figures," said Carson.

"You always a smart-ass?" asked Mike.

"Better than bein' a dumb-ass. Jeeps are better, my mom gots a new one. One of her boyfriends bought it for her."

Mike raised an eyebrow. "*One* of her boyfriends?"

"Hell yeah, pimp, get down with what's up. An' another one bought us the mobile home, an' another one bought us the swim-min' pool."

"That's nice," said Mike again. The kid really pissed him off... but he had a swimming pool. "You have any brothers or sisters?"

"I murdered 'em all," said Carson. "Eliminated the competition. Popped a cap in their bitch ho asses an' made 'em sleep with the fishes.

16

Then I cut off their heads with a chain saw an' drank their blood with fava beans an' a nice chianti. Then I chopped 'em into pieces, burned the bodies an' buried the evidence. Then I said a prayer to Satan an' stuck a bunch of pins in a doll."

"Didn't that piss off your mom?"

"I told her they ran away an' went to Hollywood. They changed their names an' became porn stars. Had sex-change operations in Sweden so she'd never recognize 'em."

"Guess you do get 200 channels."

"I'm gonna be a porn star," said Carson. "An' have a bunch of rich boyfriends."

"Um?" asked Mike. "Are you gay?"

"Nah. But rich gay boys will buy me stuff."

"Why not rich girls?" asked Mike.

"Boys are more desperate. That's what mom says." Carson made some kind of face that might have been meant to look alluring but reminded Mike of a baby with gas. "Bet I could get you to buy me stuff."

"I'll never get that desperate," said Mike.

"Give it time. ...Gots any games?"

"A few," said Mike.

"X-rated ones?"

"No!" Mike was really getting pissed... but Carson had a swim-ming pool.

Carson revved his engine. "I'll *cummm* over later an' check 'em out. I ran outta smokes, an' since you don't... which is pretty retarded... I gotta go to the store. I usually drive my Hummer, but it's in the shop this week gettin' new thumpers installed."

Mike turned toward the distant store and frowned. "They sell you cigarettes?"

"Sure, why not, they need the business. But they won't sell me beer, an' I wanted to get real drunk today. Nothin' else to do in this suckhole."

"Not even with 200 channels?" asked Mike.

"I seen it all before."

"You could go swimming," suggested Mike.

"I dropped my Ipod in the water when I was jackin'-off yester-day. I lay on a air raft an' do it a lot." Carson reached under his belly and seemed to search for something. "I might let you watch if you pay me."

"That would be desperate," said Mike.

"Ever have an erection lastin' over four hours?"

"...Maybe when I was your age."

"I'll stop on the way back," said Carson. "Maybe you'll change your mind."

"I doubt," said Mike.

"Gots a computer?"

"Yeah, a Mac."

"PCs are better. I gots a new Dell."

"Let me guess, one of your mom's..."

"Hell, yeah. You gots an Ipod?"

"Yeah."

"Can I borrow it?"

"It's still packed."

"That sucks. Well, see ya later, pimp. When I *cummm* back to check out your games."

"What about swimming?" asked Mike.

"Could happen, homes... if you're nice to me. An' my crib's air-conditioned. Gots 220 refrigerated, freeze the balls off a polar bear."

"Okay," said Mike.

"See ya, mac-daddy."

"Um?" asked Mike, as Carson throttled up his engine. "Anybody else live around here?"

"Just that rattlesnake by your foot."

"...SHIT!"

Carson laughed. "Never jump, fool. Just stand still. ...See, you made it coil up an' rattle. Now it's pissed at you."

"...Aren't you going to shoot it?"

"Why? It ain't pissed at me."

"...Um... what should I do?"

"Kiss your ass goodbye."

"That's not funny, asshole!"

"I thought it was... asshole. Just stand there an' it'll go away. It

18

can't stay out in the sun very long. ...Hey, what if it bit my dick? Then you'd have to suck it."

"Oh shut up!" Mike forced himself to stand very still when every instinct screamed to run. Watching the rattling snake, he asked, "So, there's nobody else around here but you?"

"I'm all you need, but..." Carson jerked his chin toward the shabby old house with the big dump truck. "There's Little Coyote."

"Little Coyote?" said Mike, wondering if something else might be about to attack, but scared to look around. He kept his eyes on the coiled snake, which had stopped rattling but was still watching him.

"He's an Indian an' you won't like him."

The snake began uncoiling slowly, and Mike was staying very still. "Why wouldn't I like him?"

"'Cause he's obese an' you hate obese people."

"I never said I hated them, I just don't want to be one."

"You gots all them muscles so you gotta hate 'em."

"...Why?"

"'Cause you do shit you don't like to do, thinkin' you're addin' years to your life." Carson thumbed his bobby chest. "But us fat dudes do what *we* like, an' that really pisses you 'healthy' dorks off, 'cause we're addin' life to our years."

Mike had never considered that. Did he really like building his body as much as working on his train? It was hard to admit a drunk little kid might have shaken his faith -- even for just a second -- like "health" was a religion and Carson had pissed in his church. Lamely he said, "You're not obese, just out of shape."

Carson patted his belly. "I'm in perfect shape for me 'cause I like who I am."

Mike's heart begin to slow down as the snake finally slithered away. It seemed stupid to argue about getting Active when standing still might have just saved his life. "How old is Little Coyote?"

"'Bout your age," said Carson. "But he don't gots a swimmin' pool, air-conditionin' an' 200 channels." Carson blinked his big blue eyes. "An' he ain't as cute as me." He scooted forward on the bike, baring more of its seat. "Wanna *cummm* with me to the store? Maybe they'll sell you beer 'cause you're black an' might pop a cap if they don't."

"I doubt," said Mike, wiping new sweat from his face as the snake glided over Carson's bare foot and disappeared across the road. "And I don't have a gun."

"Thought you gangstuh thugs packed steel."

"You watch way too much TV."

"They gots a few games at the store, an' a lotta good shit to eat. You can start buyin' me stuff."

Mike was tempted to go, thinking of air-conditioning and an-other 16 ounce soda... after this shit he deserved one! But, what if he got pissed at Carson -- more than he already was -- and had to walk back in this heat? ...With vultures watching him. "Nah... but thanks. I have to start unpacking and set up my weights."

"Weights are for losers who don't like themselves; an' muscles don't make 'em more likeable."

"You basically said that already," said Mike.

"But you don't believe it yet. ...I gots a new Wi."

"Let me guess," said Mike.

"Or duh! If they're nice to me, mom's nice to them, so I play 'em a lot." Carson revved his engine again and burned away in a cloud of blue smoke, spewing more dust over Mike. "*Hasta luego*, homeboy!"

Mike watched him go with very mixed feelings. A few minutes ago this had been an adventure like Indiana Jones & Son, but now he was stuck in a desert suckhole with no one around but a smart-ass kid and some Indian dude named Little Coyote... who was allegedly obese and didn't have a swimming pool.

He gazed down the road at Carson's dust. Maybe he should ride to the store? Carson was better than having no friends. ...And he had air-conditioning. Plus a swimming pool. Maybe if he took it slow he could get there and not have a heat stroke. He searched the sky for vultures, but maybe Carson had scared them off... he'd probably make an unhealthy meal, even for a vulture.

Mike walked back to the house, warily scanning for snakes on the way. ...Then he thought he saw a shadow dart away from the door. ...A dog? ...Or something else that might want to kill him? He froze, wishing he had a gun, but nothing was there. ...Probably just a heat ghost.

His jeans were soaked with sweat again -- after almost stepping on a snake he was lucky that's all they were soaked with -- so he peeled them off in the living room. He drank another hot bottle of water to prime himself for the ride to the store, then donned his last pair of fresh jeans, left the house, mounted his bike, and pedaled slowly down the road. A horned-toad scuttled out of his way, and he saw another snake... which fortunately didn't rattle or he would have fled for home.

FOUR

Little Coyote's house wasn't much bigger than Mike's, but looked at least a century older. Its sun-blasted boards had never known paint and were starkly eroded by windblown sand into ridges and gullies; but Mike was amazed by the dump truck... it really *was* almost as big as the house! Its dual rear tires were six feet tall, and even the smaller tires in front were twice the size of an 18-wheeler's. There were no side panels on its long hood, and the engine was also awesomely huge. The radiator was guarded by mesh that looked strong enough to head-butt a tank; but the vehicle also looked very old, like something from the 1930s, its yellow paint chalky and faded with patches of orange rust all over like some gigantic Tonka toy forgotten in a kid's sandbox... a kid from *Gulliver's Travels* in the land of giants.

Mike stopped to study the mammoth machine after checking the road for snakes. Like most boys who'd played with Tonkas, it was like a dream come true... even if too late for him. Then he noticed someone underneath in the massive vehicle's lake of shade who seemed to be pumping a grease gun like his father did on the Rover.

Mike squinted against the sun glare... if that was "Little" Coyote, the truck was a Matchbox toy! The truck's ground clearance was at least three feet, and the dude seemed to need every inch of that as he wiggled and wallowed around in the dirt applying the gun to various fittings. Mike couldn't see him very well... except that he was **FAT!**

The boy didn't seem to have noticed Mike, busy with his greasy work, and Mike was tempted to just ride on. He could be "nice" to Carson -- up to a non-perverted point -- if it got him into that swim-

22

ming pool and under refrigerated air, but what could he possibly have in common with anyone who was *that* obese?

He watched the enormous boy at work beneath the titanic truck. He really didn't hate fat kids – after all, he'd almost been one and had never felt any less of a person because he'd weighed a little more -- mostly these days he felt sorry for them because they got dissed and hated by assholes. And, of course, they weren't healthy. But, maybe Carson had been right and only losers ended up here?

He hesitated, one foot on a pedal. On the other hand, this huge fat dude was the only other boy in the 'hood. He probably wasn't very smart -- no one *that* obese could be -- but maybe his mind was cleaner than Carson's. And, at least he was getting Active instead of playing video games.

The sun blazed down on Mike's ebony skin, and he'd probably sweated two bottles of water and maybe more already. He glanced at the store, a half-mile closer, thinking of air-conditioning and chug-ging a liter of icy Coke. His dad would be coming back in an hour and would probably stop for beer, so even if he got pissed at Carson he wouldn't have to ride home on his bike.

Then a voice called, "Hi."

Almost feeling trapped somehow, Mike returned the greeting, his dry throat turning it into a croak. He walked his bike to the gigantic truck while the super-size boy wallowed out from under, reminding Mike of a blubbery seal undulating across a beach.

The dude wore only jeans and sneaks, though he hardly "wore" the jeans at all, more than half baring a mammoth bottom like two copper planets colliding, and overhung by the rolls of his waist as he finally got to his feet... a process that took half a minute and made Mike instinctively want to help. Mike had never seen so much fat... at least on a kid! The dude's vast belly hung down to his knees, with a navel like a railroad tunnel, and he had to lean drastically backward to balance all that pendulous bulk, which jiggled and quivered with every move like the cliché about Jell-O. His boy-breasts were bulbously bulging balloons that looked on the verge of exploding, and he had more rolls than a Shar-pei puppy. He wasn't any taller than Mike – which somehow seemed surprising -- though at least three times as big around, his upper arms twice the size of Mike's thighs, and must have weighed almost five-hundred pounds.

Which meant he was a hundred-pound boy carrying four-hundred pounds... a concept that awed Mike a little.

He was old-penny copper all over, though further darkened by rust-colored dirt, and his ragged jeans looked more like leather blackly soaked with oil. They drooped dangerously low on gargan-tuan hips; and only the toes of his tattered sneaks showed beneath their tumbled cuffs. His hair was also black and oily, cascading over the orbs of his chest and halfway down his rolly back, though partly tamed by a red bandana. His triple-chinned face was as round as a moon, with cheeks that engulfed a small button nose; and his eyes were shiny obsidian, though all but hidden under his hair. His scent matched his size but was not really bad -- mostly very earthy boy -- though he wasn't sweating much, at least compared to Mike. Nor was he panting like Mike despite the struggle of getting up. His smile was open and friendly, which, at least where Mike came from, usually meant a short-bus kid; though Mike couldn't see enough of his eyes to confirm what he suspected.

But nobody cool would have gotten *that* fat!

The dude had already said hi, and Mike's reply didn't count. A slow kid would have babbled, eagerly offering all he had in hope of making a friend, but it seemed up to Mike to make the next move.

"Little Coyote?" said Mike.

"At your service," said the dude, offering a fat-padded paw displaying dimples instead of knuckles, the grease gun still in the other. "I saw you meeting Carson."

"Mike," said Mike. Little Coyote's tremendous belly made it awkward to get close enough for a shake; and then it wasn't really a shake, only a strong but very brief grip. Yet, he felt as if Little Coyote had gotten a lot of data like a contact spirit reading. Then the dude, though still looking friendly, didn't offer anything else... which, Mike had to admit, was cool.

Not knowing their relationship, it wouldn't be cool to dis Carson. Or maybe not to dis him. "I just moved into the house up the road." That was uncool babble, but maybe cooler than nothing.

24

"I saw you," Little Coyote said in a matter-of-fact tone of voice, the same as his previous statement.

Mike caught himself before saying "um" and raised his eyes to the truck. "That's cool," he said. "What is it?"

That might have deserved, "a truck," but Little Coyote went on smiling. "A Euclid."

"Never heard of those," said Mike.

"Don't feel bad, most people haven't. They were made for mines and quarries. This is a 1947 with a Cummins 220 engine."

"Cool," said Mike, and it kind of was. He walked around to the back of the truck, noting only one tail light, ruby glass and tiny. Up close he couldn't see into the bed because it was so high off the ground, but he'd seen from the road it was empty, and totally red with rust.

"Hauls twenty tons," said Little Coyote, laying his gun on the truck's running-board.

"Cool," said Mike, impressed. "So it runs?"

"Sure. I cleaned the injectors and rebuilt the pump. Changed all the oil and filters, and put on new belts and hoses."

"Cool," said Mike again, understanding some of that from help-ing his dad on the Rover. "What do you use it for?"

"Cruising and going to the store."

Mike studied the dude but he looked on the real. He was won-dering whether to ask what it cost when Little Coyote went on:

"I knew your great-uncle Joseph. He told me about you and your dad."

"I never met him," said Mike.

"He always hoped you'd come out here someday."

"Makes me kinda sad," said Mike. Then, though it seemed a bit morbid, he added, "...Um... did he...?"

"Die in the house?"

"...Yeah," said Mike.

"Peacefully in his sleep. He was a hundred-and-seven, so it pro-bably didn't surprise him."

"We never knew how old he was." Mike turned back to regard the truck, and Little Coyote said:

"They were gonna scrap it when they shut down the copper mine."

"That was retarded," said Mike.

"Go figure," said Little Coyote. "But I used to help in the shop up there, and the foreman said if I could get it home he'd forget about it."

"Cool," said Mike, admiring the tires, at least a foot taller than he, though obviously ancient and heavily scarred.

"I needed something to get around, and I'm way too fat for a minibike."

Mike glanced at Little Coyote again, but he only seemed to be stating a fact, not dissing himself before someone else did like a lot of fat kids had learned to do. Mike almost suggested losing weight, but said instead, "It fits you, man."

Little Coyote patted his belly, making it ripple in waves, its cavernous navel aimed earthward and far below the reach of his hands. "Figured you'd notice sooner or later."

"...Um, guess it don't bother you?"

Little Coyote grinned. "What?"

Mike laughed, and turned to the truck again, pushing up his cap to see it all at once. "It's kinda like a huge model."

"You build models?"

"Had an H.O. train layout, but then I got my weights."

"It shows."

"Figured you'd notice sooner or later."

"Building a model of Mike?"

"...Kinda, I guess," said Mike, though he'd never considered that.

"I build ships, want to see 'em?"

"Sure."

Little Coyote waddled to the house in kind of a ponderous penguin-like gait, each step seeming a major event, sort of bull-dozing his belly along, which wobbled and wallowed against huge thighs that seemed to get in each other's way, the balloons of his boy-breasts bobbing and bouncing, the rest of his body rippling and quaking. Mike followed, again feeling something like awe since it seemed against the laws of physics for all that fat to be ambulatory, much less propelled by a thirteen-year-old. He remembered last year when his own puppy chub – as his dad cheerfully called it -- had also wobbled around when he'd walked, his belly lolling over his jeans, his boy-breasts bobbing softly about. His body had felt kind of – friendly -- back then, like a comfortable place to be.

Little Coyote laboriously mounted a single sagging plank step and crossed a creakingly protesting porch to open a squeaky screen door.

"Your parents home?" asked Mike, then wondered if that was cool, since he didn't have plural parents.

"Just got a big sister," said Little Coyote. "'Rents in the Happy Hunting Ground."

"...Oh, sorry," said Mike.

"It was a long time ago. Crashed their car but saved a coyote."

"Still sorry," said Mike.

"It's not all bad, the coyotes owe me."

"...Oh," said Mike, supposing it was an Indian thing.

"My sister's at work," Little Coyote added. "She cooks at the Coyote Cafe in town." He pointed to the distant highway. "Truckers get off the Interstate and take this old valley road; come thirty miles out of their way just to eat her cooking."

"Guess she rules the range," said Mike.

"Hey, that's good."

"What tribe are you?"

"Apache. And you?"

"...Orphan African, I guess."

"We're a little luckier, the whitemen just stole our land and didn't brain-wipe our memories."

The house was built to an ancient style, with tongue-and-groove walls and lofty ceilings, the latter plated with patterned tin. The tube-and-post wiring had probably been added in the 1920s. There didn't seem to be air-conditioning, but the house, though hot, was cooler than Mike's, and curtains tamed the savage sun, making it shadowy inside. The living room was surprisingly neat -- though Mike wondered why that surprised him -- and simply furnished in what he supposed was desert Native-American. Indian blankets -- naturally -- covered most of the walls, along with an old-fashioned couch and chair, both of which showed sagging signs of Little Coyote's size. There

27

was a small TV, and a 1970s stereo with a stack of eight-track tapes – The Stones, The Doors, Pavlov's Dog, Blue Oyster Cult, REO Speedwagon, Boston, Styx, and Bad Company -- along with a pair of kerosene lamps that were obviously more than decorations. There were lots of beads and feathers, and a colorful -- Navajo? -- rug on the floor. Several bone-white animal skulls, maybe dogs' -- or coyotes' -- seemed to watch Mike with long-vanished eyes. The skulls made him think of something.

"Um... when my great-uncle died...?"

"The coyotes told me," said Little Coyote. "A bunch of them came to sing him good-bye, so he didn't decompose in the house."

"Just sorta wondered," said Mike.

"I called Doc Millburn, and me and my sister stayed till he came. He's the undertaker, too." Little Coyote smiled. "Your uncle isn't haunting the place."

"How did you know I...?"

"Logical progression of thought."

"Did you lock the windmill?"

"You're kidding, right? I told Carson to do it."

"Oh. Thanks."

"I saw you climbing up to unlock it."

"Yeah, but the tank's all shrunk."

"It'll leak for a few days. Come over for water anytime. Our tank holds two-thousand gallons so we've always got plenty."

"Thanks. ...Did this used to be water stop? I saw old railroad tracks from up there."

"Yeah. For the Coyote Valley And Codyville Railroad."

There were many shelves of books taking up almost a wall by themselves, which also surprised Mike a little. He paused to scan the titles: lots of old-time stories for boys from the early 1900s when boys had adventures and invented things -- *The Aeroplane Boys, The Motor Boys, The Steam Boys*, and many others -- plus Dickens, Poe, and Hemingway, Steinbeck, Flannery O'Connor, H.P. Lovecraft, Lewis Carroll, Ralph Ellison, and Thorne Smith. There were also many sea stories; *Moby Dick*, all the Hornblower books, *We Didn't Mean To Go To Sea, Typhoon, Captains Courageous, Ghost Ship*...

A shadow moved at the edge of Mike's sight, seeming to slip behind the couch. "You have a dog?" he asked.

Little Coyote gave him a curious look. "Did you see one?"

"...Guess not," said Mike.

Little Coyote led the way down a hall barely wide enough for his middle, the floorboards creaking loudly. A doorway showed a tiny bathroom similar to the one in Mike's house, with a high-tank toilet and tin shower stall. Little Coyote couldn't have fit in the stall, which seemed to explain his earthy boy scent.

They came to another doorway, and Mike saw a kitchen with a wood-burning range, though there was also a microwave. And the fridge looked like a commercial model of gleaming stainless-steel. Brightly polished copper pots and blackened iron frying pans hung from hooks on doorless cupboards stacked with plates, bowls and cups with colorful designs. Dried red peppers hung from a nail, and there was a shelf of Mason jars containing herbs and spices. None of the jars were labeled; but who would need a label if they knew what they were doing? Little Coyote's sister obviously loved to cook... the progression of thought was obvious.

"Want a Coke?" asked Little Coyote.

"Yeah, thanks," said Mike, who felt like he could slam a gallon... no matter how unhealthy that was.

The house's interior doorways were narrow, built before any codes, and Little Coyote squeezed himself through to open one of the fridge's doors.

LARD!

...came bellowing out at Mike like someone yelling fuck in a church. There was a gallon can of the stuff, and it wasn't ashamed of its label! Mike stared in shocked fascination as if actually meeting the fabled Satan the god of health had warned him about.

It was hard to see around Little Coyote -- there was a lot to see around -- but the fridge had a lot of unhealthy food, though Mike himself drank real milk and not the milk-flavored water crap they made kids drink at school. ...And the sixers of San Miguel beer were cool. ...And there were fruits and vegetables; apples, oranges, limes and lettuce, onions, tomatoes and avocados. And a lot of cheese. Coke was only naughty to Mike... a very minor apprentice imp com-pared to Satan LARD.

But, Gansitos were DEVIL'S FOOD that made you fat just looking at them and thinking -- in Mike's case remembering -- how goddamn good they tasted.

The sour-cream was enticingly evil, making him think of big juicy tacos -- something else he'd given up -- and so was badass butter, reminding him of his dad's pancakes... of which he partook only sparingly now. But his eyes were always drawn to LARD, like a porno site that didn't pretend to be anything but what it was.

"Ground control to Major Mike." Little Coyote offered a bottle of Coke, the old-school style from Mexico.

"...Oh, thanks."

"Looked like you were having a vision."

"...I'm kinda tired," said Mike, yanking his eyes away from LARD, which seemed to smirk like Carson. "We drove all night. And I'm not used to this heat."

"Yeah, you should take it slow at first. Mad dogs and English-men...'"

"I've read that," said Mike, and wiped sweat from his face. "But now I really know what it means."

"Want a beer instead? The sun's sufficiently over the yardarm."

"Sure," said Mike, then laughed. "At least I got part of my wish."

"What was the rest of it?" Little Coyote asked, taking out two frosty bottles and handing one to Mike.

"...Just... kind of a daydream," said Mike, popping the cap and gratefully gulping.

"Careful what you wish for; the universe has a sense of humor." Little Coyote indicated a platter covered with aluminum foil. "You had lunch? My sister made beef and cheese burritos. I already ate, but there's two left. I can nuke 'em if you want."

"...I... don't normally eat lunch," said Mike.

Little Coyote raised an eyebrow, though only half seen under his hair. "What's normal about that?"

"We had breakfast at a truck stop about four o'clock this morn-ing."

"The Buddhists say, 'when hungry eat, when tired sleep.'"

"...Guess I could eat one," said Mike.

Little Coyote took out the platter and unwrapped the foil, revealing a pair of enormous burritos, golden-brown and tempting as hell... even if they'd been made with LARD. "Only one?"

"...Yeah."

"Want sour cream?"

"...Um... sure."

Little Coyote slipped the platter into the microwave. "I'll join you, it's a long time till supper."

Little Coyote's den was also well supplied with books, their titles very eclectic, from *The Wind In The Willows* to *Portnoy's Complaint*, including *The Hobbit* and *Lord Of The Rings*, along with *The Jungle Book* and *Kim*. It smelled like Little Coyote -- a lot -- but there was a lot of him; and the bed was braced with railroad ties. There weren't any sheets, just Indian blankets. Judging from the dude's ragged jeans, it wasn't surprising there weren't many clothes -- they wouldn't be cheap in his size -- and there wasn't a dresser. The only garments in evidence were a clean pair of jeans on a dynamite box and a blanket poncho draped on a hook. Maybe, being an Indian, he didn't wear shirts or socks? And, it was already obvious that shorts weren't part of his wardrobe.

There was a dog -- or coyote -- skull adorned with feathers on a wall, and a kerosene lamp on a box by the bed... another dynamite box. For sound there was only a small radio; for the Web an elderly Imac. A Winchester carbine, an old Yellow Boy, rested on pegs on another wall. It looked well-oiled and ready to shoot. Also not surprising, thanks to western movies, were the hawk feathers tied to its barrel.

"Great-grandfather fought for his freedom with that," said Little Coyote, tracking Mike's eyes. "Unfortunately..."

"He lost," said Mike.

Little Coyote smiled. "In your case gaining muscles didn't mean losing your mind."

"They don't have to be mutually-exclusive," said Mike. "Just like..."

31

Little Coyote laughed. "I'll take that as a compliment."

The models were crazy awesome! All over the room were model ships filling homemade shelves, all beautifully built and perfectly painted. There was everything from clipper ships to freighters and ocean liners, including a huge *Titanic.*

"These are way past cool!" exclaimed Mike, a burrito half-eaten in one hand, a near-empty San Miguel in the other; though, despite Little Coyote's obvious intelligence, it was still hard to believe this huge fat boy could have built them, those chubby paws had painted them, or could have done such delicate work. ...Or maybe it was hard to believe that under all that tangled hair and inside all that awesome fat was someone who could do it. Sure, he could fix a big brutal truck, but rig a tiny sailing ship with lines as fine as spiderweb? Mike walked around saying "cool!" a lot, but then asked, "Why ships in the desert?"

"I like the ocean."

"...Oh. Ever been there?"

"Nah, but maybe someday."

Mike felt sad for a moment, imagining Little Coyote on a Cali-fornia beach and all the retarded hate he would get from assholes who only saw his size.

Another ship was being built, a steam freighter on a table at the room's single window. Mike leaned close to study it, but Little Coyote tapped his shoulder.

"There's a telephone truck in front of your house."

Mike peered out the window, squinting against the sun glare. "Guess I better go before it gets away."

"Yeah, they're elusive out here. Want to come over later?"

"Yeah," said Mike, realizing he did... even without a swimming pool, air-conditioning and 200 channels.

FIVE

The telephone man was just climbing down from the sun-shriveled pole as Mike rolled up to a gasping stop with sweat pouring off his body and spattering the dusty road like tiny atomic explosions.

Despite his orange hard-hat and well-equipped tool belt, the man looked like an old prospector in a western movie -- deeply tanned and leathery-faced, with a bristle of grizzled whiskers -- though the Remington six-shooter also helped. "You must be new to the desert, son. Slow down if you want to live to enjoy it."

Mike almost asked what there was to enjoy, but the man smiled in a friendly way. "Don't have to worry 'bout gettin' sunburned?"

"Actually I do," said Mike, pushing up his cap a little. "Just not as much, but I'll get darker."

"You get much darker, folks'll have to look twice to see you once. But don't be takin' that wrong, son. I served in 'Nam with a lot of Brothers... that was the word in the '60s. Fact is, I wouldn't be here today 'cept for a Brother buddy of mine. Took out a Charlie before he got me."

"Um, cool," said Mike, not knowing what else to say, but feeling a little relieved. Every contact was a first contact when meeting white people, he'd found.

The man sat down on the truck's running-board to take off his climbing spikes... the truck was a Chevrolet 4X4 from the early 1960s, and didn't seem to have AC because its cab windows were open. "Knew your great-uncle real well. Figured you was the nephew he talked about a lot. Had a picture of you in his room."

"I am," said Mike.

33

The man studied Mike. "Hope you ain't been sick; looks like you lost a lotta weight since that picture was taken."

"Um, no," said Mike. "Guess it was an older picture from when I used to be chubby last year."

"Always hopin' to meet you, he was."

"Too bad that never happened," said Mike. "My dad always wanted me to meet him, but we couldn't afford to drive here when gas got so expensive. And I guess there isn't a train."

"Not since 1920 when the Santa Fe pulled up its spur." The man got up and put his spikes into one of the truck's compartments. "Real good man, your uncle was. Folks 'round here all liked him. Last of the real ol'-timers from back when there was still a railroad runnin' over them mountains."

"To a ghost town?" asked Mike. "Codyville?"

The man sat down again and pulled a pack of Bugler tobacco from a pocket of his blue work shirt. He offered it to Mike, who politely declined, then started to roll a cigarette. "Wasn't a ghost town then, son. Real boomin' place in its day... had churches, a school, an' a library. Even had a movie house in its later years. Had a good reputation, too. Not like Bodie in California or a lotta them other 'ol minin' towns full of claim-jumpers, back-shooters an' thieves... had a real good sheriff." The man pointed north-east. "Gold came outta them mines up there for almost thirty years. Coyote Valley an' Codyville train hauled it down to Coyote Flats to meet the Santa Fe, an' there was only one robbery ever happened in all that time. June of 1897."

"Did the robbers get caught?" asked Mike.

The man lit his smoke with a wooden match scratched on the running-board. "That was the only crime the Codyville sheriff never solved... tho' he swore he'd never rest till he did. There was close to a ton of gold bars stolen off the train. ...'Bout a mile west from the feet of them mountains. Wasn't nobody shot or killed: the robbers... four of 'em, there was... tied up the train crew in the caboose an' loaded the gold in a big ore wagon. Then they rolled off into the night, an' wasn't never seen again! Only one road leadin' outta this valley, an' that was watched by deputies... every wagon an' saddlebag searched before they let 'em through the pass. An' they searched every person, box, trunk an' suitcase goin' out on the Santa Fe. Them bars weighed almost thirty pounds each... twenty-seven somethin', I think... so they wasn't easy to carry or hide. The insurance company posted a ten-thousand dollar reward... lotta money back then, son... hired some Pinkerton's men, an' kept the search goin' for over a year, while the Codyville sheriff kept deputies watchin', but none of that gold was ever found."

"Woah!" said Mike. "How much is a ton of gold worth?"

"Never been a whiz at math, son, but gold was about twenty dollars an ounce in 1897. ...That's troy weight, twelve ounces a pound. Makes two-hundred an' forty dollars for a pound of gold, but after that it gets fuzzy to me."

Mike considered. "The bars weighed almost thirty pounds each... call it thirty to keep it simple. ...That would be... um... seven-thousand, two-hundred dollars just for one bar!" He thought for another moment. "There's two-thousand pounds in a ton..."

"Two-thousand, four-hundred an' somethin' in a troy ton," the man corrected.

"I'd need a calculator," said Mike. "But that's a *lot* of money!"

The man puffed out a ghost of smoke. "Over a half million dollars in 1897."

"Woah!" said Mike again. "What about today?"

"Gold's over a thousand dollars an ounce."

"WOAH!" exclaimed Mike. "And nobody ever found it?"

"Not that I ever heard tell. ...'Course, there's a lotta stories."

"Like, what?" asked Mike.

"Take a seat in the shade, son... that's somethin' you need to learn 'bout the desert, only 'get active' when you have to." The man indicated the running-board, and Mike sat down beside him. "Some said the robbers buried their wagon, maybe in some ol' mine shaft rigged with a dynamite charge, an' rode away on the horses, plannin' to come back an' dig it out after the fuss died down. But they didn't figure the Codyville sheriff wasn't gonna give up on the case. Even after the insurance paid off, he kept a watch 'round the robbery site till Codyville turned up its toes in 1917... along with him, they say."

The man exhaled another ghost. "A lot can happen in twenty years, so maybe the robbers were dead by then... pretty short lifespan back in them days if you was on the wrong side of the law out here in the west. Other folks said the Indians musta ambushed 'em an' took the gold. 'Pay-back' for their land bein' stolen. ...Used to be a village out there, but the government run 'em off to clear the way for minin'."

"What do you think happened?" asked Mike.

"Never give it much thought myself... guess I'm immune to gold fever. But your great-uncle always maintained that gold is still here in this valley, an' likely not far from the ol' railroad tracks."

"Why did he think that?" asked Mike.

The man took another puff. "The robbery happened just after midnight... full moon, it was, so the story goes. They'd made it look like the wagon was stuck on the tracks to stop the train. After they'd tied up the crew an' busted open the boxcar door, it took 'em a while to load the wagon... maybe an hour all told. The engineer got himself loose about an hour later. After untyin' his fireman, the brakeman an' conductor, he high-balled into Coyote Flats. Their sheriff formed up a posse; they loaded their horses onto the train, an' were back at the scene of the crime at dawn... 'round about six that mornin'. Which only left the robbers about five hours to get away. An' a wagon with a ton of gold couldn't have got very far."

The man paused for another puff. "Assumin' they wasn't idiots, they woulda known there wasn't much time to make a getaway. Even if the engineer hadn't got himself untied, the railroad woulda sent a crew to look for the train when it didn't arrive in Coyote Flats. ...That's why a lot of people figured they'd planned to bury the wagon. The train went on up to Codyville, an' by noon came back with their sheriff an' another posse. They spread out an' searched all day, but it was like that wagon an' gold had vanished into the Twilight Zone! Wasn't even no wheel tracks to show which way they'd gone."

"Woah!" said Mike again.

The man chuckled. "Kinda 'far out,' like we used to say. That's why some people figured the Indians got the gold... *they* could do somethin' like that. Even heard tales the coyotes helped by coverin' up the wagon tracks. ...'Course, there's supernatural theories;

everything from UFOs, to Indian spirits takin' revenge."

"Did people keep looking?" asked Mike.

"A few were still lookin' when I was your age, but the story never spread very far... not like the tale of the Lost Dutchman Mine... an' it's pretty much been forgotten; tho' your great-uncle kept on lookin' almost up to the day he died."

"Wish I could have met him," said Mike.

The man flipped his cigarette away. "We all have regrets about things in the past, things we did or didn't do an' wish we didn't or did, but sometimes that wasn't our fault... situations beyond our control, or not knowin' then what we learned later on."

"I guess so," said Mike. "Thanks for telling me the story."

"The desert's full of stories, son, for those who got the sense to listen." The man pulled a clipboard out of the cab. "You're all hooked up, sign right here."

"Will my computer work on this system?" The aluminum clipboard was blistering hot, though the man didn't seem to have noticed.

"Gonna get lucky in one of them chat rooms?"

"Hasn't happened yet," said Mike, gingerly signing the form.

"You'll only get about 2800 bps on this wire. These lines were put up in '33."

"Guess I'll have to live with that."

"You could get satellite service."

"Yeah, but I guess that's expensive. ...What about the power?"

"Sorry, son, I just do phones. But now you can call an' find out."

"Yeah. Thanks."

The man tore off a copy and gave it to Mike. "Don't depend on electricity, son; this heat plays hell with the transformers." He tilted back his hard-hat and frowned up at the pole. "That one's in a bad way now. I'll report it for you, but the power company won't do nothin' till it finally blows, an' then they'll take their time." He glanc-ed at the big mobile home up the road. "Miss Kitty's place is all electric, includin' the water pump, but that pool gives 'em a backup."

"*Miss* Kitty?" asked Mike.

"Kitty Russel. You acquainted?"

37

"I met her son awhile ago."

"Oh, I get 'cha. Carson's a cactus-colt all right, but ain't no shame in that no more... 'least to decent folks."

"Guess not," said Mike.

"You gotta roll with the changes, son. Or they'll roll right over you."

"Yeah, I've noticed that."

"Come mid-summer, the power will go off a lot out here, an' might stay off for days at a time. You got plenty of water?"

"I unlocked the windmill," said Mike.

"Won't be no breeze till after sundown, an' it's gonna take a while before your tank fills up. Ask Little Coyote for help if you need it... seen you ridin' in from his place so I reckon you got acquainted. Desert folks look out for each other, an' what he don't know about the desert ain't worth the bother of learnin'." The man offered a hand. "Name's Bert Walker, I'm in the book. Call me if you need any-thing Little Coyote can't help you with. ...'Course, it'll take me a while to get here, I'm twenty miles across the valley."

Mike shook the tough old hand. "Mike Saunders. And thanks."

"Pleased to meet you, Mike. ...An' watch out for rattlesnakes, we got a lot of 'em here."

"Why don't you kill some?" asked Mike.

"Back in the ol' days that's just what we done... shot 'em on sight like coyotes. The Indians said we was fools, an' turned out they was right... pretty soon this whole valley was overrun with rats an' mice. Them rodents carry diseases that'll kill you as dead as a rattlesnake bite an' a lot more slower an' painful. An, rattlesnakes don't infest your house, eat your food an' chew up your things, an' poop all over the place. An' they'll leave you alone if you give 'em a choice. After all, you're too big to eat so they only bite defendin' themselves."

"What about coyotes?" asked Mike.

"They never really bothered nobody, not around here with no cattle or sheep, tho' they'll go after your chickens."

"I don't think we're gonna have chickens," said Mike. "...So, I shouldn't be scared of coyotes?"

"Never heard of a coyote attackin' nobody."

"What about vultures?"

Bert laughed. "They ain't gonna bother you till you're dead, an' then you ain't gonna care. An' watch where you step, 'specially at night, an' you won't have no trouble with Mr. Rattle. Got a snake-bite kit just in case?"

"My dad bought one at the store."

"Want a Coke?"

"Sure. ...Yes please."

Bert pulled a bottle out of an ice chest on the truck's dusty seat. "Thanks," said Mike, gulping it down. Then he asked after muffling a burp, "Should I get a gun? Everybody else seems to have one."

"Out here it's better to have a gun, even if you don't need it, than to need a gun an' not have one." Bert reached into the cab again and brought out a short, double-barrel shotgun, the old-fashioned kind with rabbit-ear hammers. "Here's a house-warmin' present, Mike. Kinda beat-up but still shoots fine. It's a ten-gauge, so it kicks like a mule."

"Thanks," said Mike, accepting the gun, which was as hot as the clipboard. "Um, is it loaded?"

"Wouldn't be much good if it weren't. ...Supposedly, it's the gun they carried on the Codyville train. Tho' it didn't do 'em no good... engineer an' fireman got down off the locomotive to help push the wagon off the tracks, an' the robbers got the drop on 'em. Same with the conductor an' brakeman in the caboose."

"Wasn't there a guard for the gold?"

"Company figured they didn't need one since there'd never been a robbery, an' there wasn't no way outta this valley 'cept the one road an' the Santa Fe. 'Sides, like I said, the gold was insured, so the company didn't lose no money. Only thing really got hurt was the Codyville sheriff's pride, tho' nobody held it against him. ...Some say his ghost is still out there tryin' to solve the crime."

"You believe in ghosts?" asked Mike.

"Lotta ghosts in the desert, son, don't matter if you believe or not. ...Here's a box of shells." He pointed toward the store. "You need any more, Griswold has 'em."

"Thanks a lot, Mr. Walker."

"Have a nice day, an' be seein' you, Mike, even if I gotta look twice."

Mike laughed. "Okay, and thanks again."

"Hope your weight gets back to normal soon." Bert got in the truck and drove off, leaving a cloud of rusty dust that settled very slowly. Everything was slow in this place.

SIX

Cradling the gun in one arm, Mike walked his bike to the house. His jeans were sodden with sweat, *déjà vu*... he'd either have to get used to that or make a pair of cut-offs like Carson's. Damn, he wanted a shower bad! A cold one in Alaska! He put the gun on the kitchen table and guzzled two bottles of water, then realized there weren't any more. But, there was a store a mile away... though it seemed like ten in this heat. Just riding back from Little Coyote's had been like working-out for an hour. He needed a minibike like Carson's... and a swimming pool. But his dad would be back any time, bringing more water and probably beer.

Taking the gun to his room, he lay it on his weight bench and stripped naked again except for his cap. Total silence ruled, and his dog-like breaths seemed unnaturally loud.

...Almost too loud. As if there was someone *else* panting with him!

It was like one of his father's stories where footsteps followed you though an old house and at first you thought they were your own... until you began to realize they went on a second after you stopped!

He held his breath but heard nothing: the panting had ceased when his had...

Or had it?

He leaned out the window and looked around... nothing but silent, shimmering desert. Little Coyote had said his great-uncle wasn't haunting the house, and Indians were supposed to know about that kind of stuff. ...But, maybe a ghost had moved in while the house was empty?

...Or, maybe some two-legged desert rat was squatting in the

41

house?

He grabbed the gun, cocked both hammers, and cautiously searched all the rooms, but there was nothing and no one. The larger bedroom had been his great-uncle's, sparsely furnished with a battered old dresser and a tarnished brass bed, both covered with dust. On the dresser was a small photograph in tin-plated frame, a print of himself taken by his dad when he'd been twelve last year, shirtless at his train layout with a can of Coke and a pack of Gansitos. Yeah, he'd been overweight, but he'd also looked happy. But he wasn't unhappy now... was he?

Finally, he returned to his room and put the gun back on the bench after letting the hammers down. How long had he been here? No more than four hours, but it felt like a year.

He suddenly wanted sound; cars driving past, a neighbor's lawn-mower, little kids yelling in grassy yards and somebody calling their dog. He dug through a box and found his Ipod... but he'd forgotten to charge it. No music, no games, no TV, no Web. ...Well, he could always read a book.

It occurred to him that reading was something you did alone. Or at least alone in your mind with only the characters in the story. He gazed around the hot silent room in the hot silent house in the hot silent desert and realized this was more alone than he'd ever been in his life.

He could go back to Little Coyote's, but that meant another ride in the heat. It was only half a mile, and in Thousand Oaks he'd jog-ged every day twice as far as that; but here it seemed like a mara-thon, and one he wasn't in shape to run. He glanced at the bench: he'd missed his workout yesterday -- the first time in nearly a year -- because they'd left at dawn. ...But, working-out seemed ridiculous when everything here was like working-out!

He thought of Little Coyote again, maybe 500 pounds and hardly sweating while working on his truck in the sun. Maybe he'd have to re-think what being in shape was really about?

Going to the kitchen, he rummaged through several boxes until he found a quart of rum. His dad always had a glass at night after a day of writing -- calling it the "spook chaser" -- and Mike often joined him with a rum-and-Coke. But now he didn't have any Coke... unless he rode ten miles to the store. He took the bottle into his room and flopped on the squeaky old bed, raising dust. Then, despite the heat, he laughed. "Some things don't need electricity." He uncapped the bottle and drank liquid fire, then closed his eyes and began.

Aside from various methods, there were two basic ways of doing it. One, Mike called the physical, usually on the spur of a moment when he simply felt the need. The other, and best, engaged his mind with a prologue of daydreams and fantasies, always when he had plenty of time. Right now he probably had an hour before his dad returned. He'd smell afterward with no way to wash, but his dad never teased him about it; so, with slow and gentle strokes, he let his mind wander to see where it went.

Gradually a vision formed... but it was very weird. For a moment he almost stopped. ...Yet, it was strangely fascinating so he continued his sensuous strokes. He saw himself tied to a totem pole, shirtless in only his jeans. His arms were bound around the pole, his hands roped together behind it.

Okay, he got the significance, both Freudian and realtime, since he'd just met Little Coyote.

But, Carson stood above him smiling impishly, a box of Gansitos in hand. Mike found he was desperately hungry -- even lustfully hungry -- and Carson was feeding him, ramming the evilly tempting and devilishly delicious cakes into his eager mouth. That was pretty Freudian, too... and in a disturbing way.

He almost stopped again... but he was so desperately hungry! And those Gansitos tasted so good!

"More!" his vision self pleaded, and Carson generously com-plied. The box seemed inexhaustible, yet Mike's hunger raged and he couldn't stop! His muscles seemed to be melting, his body revert-ing into the shape he'd been a year ago, his pecs becoming soft and round, his belly rapidly fattening and rolling over the top of his jeans.

And still he wanted more!

And the strangest thing was... *he liked it!*

And so did his physical form on the bed. He couldn't stop in either sense.

Somebody snickered.

Mike's eyes snapped open. For an instant he'd thought of a smart-ass ghost, but Carson stood in the doorway.

"THE HELL ARE YOU DOING IN HERE!" bawled Mike.

"I said I was *cummmin'* back. Think I was bustin' your crappy-ass crib?" Carson studied Mike. "Thought it would be bigger."

"Stereotype," said Mike, who considered himself a bit above average... at least for his age. He hadn't heard the minibike... but he'd been somewhere else.

"Wanna see mine?" asked Carson.

"No," said Mike. "...And I should charge you."

"I wasn't watchin' that long. Let's do a twosome an' call it even."

"No!"

"That don't mean you'd be gay."

"I know that, dammit. ...Here, have a drink."

"Cool!" said Carson and padded over, his bare feet making potato-chip sounds in the gritty carpet of dust. Like many out of shape kids, he'd never developed his abs to support his belly blub-ber, which wobbled and plunged with every step. It hid his cut-offs in a frontal view, and his slouching-backward posture made him look like he was following it, while the barrel of his cartoon cannon al-most dragged the floor... which could have been Freudian, too. "I brung you a Coke, we can drink it with that."

He uncapped a 16 ounce bottle, took a monster gulp of rum and chased it with a guzzle of Coke. "That rocks! Here, try it."

Mike did. "Yeah, it's good that way."

"Can I smoke?"

"Hell... Oh, go ahead."

"Ain't you scared of second-hand smoke?"

Mike drank more rum. "I have scarier things to be scared of."

"Like gettin' obese?"

"It's just rum and Coke."

"I brung you a double cheeseburger, too, but I'll eat it if you're scared of it."

"I'm not scared of it, dammit!" Mike realized he was hungry, despite Little Coyote's monster burrito, and eagerly unwrapped the burger. He'd forgotten how good burgers tasted, even convenience store microwave types... no matter how unhealthy they were.

Carson pulled out a pack of Camels, the old-school unfiltered kind, and fired one with an ancient brass Zippo. Then he plopped on the bed beside Mike. "This is like a porno flick."

"Not till you came in," said Mike, his mouth full of juicy meat and cheese, which rivaled his vision Gansitos.

Carson blew a smoke ring. "You're gonna love me."

"Look," said Mike. "I'm not gay... not that there's anything wrong with that."

"Not if they buy you stuff," said Carson, taking another drink.

"You just bought me stuff," said Mike.

Carson shrugged. "I was bein' nice. An' you better be nice to me 'cause I'm all you gots."

"Little Coyote is cool."

"Yeah, but he's obese."

"Don't call him that; it sounds like nigga without the A... which I guess it's supposed to."

Carson blinked his big blue eyes. "I'm a lot cuter."

"Only 'cause some people say you are... the 'dominant race'... but I don't have to agree with them."

"Yeah?" snapped Carson. "You're black as a...!"

"Telephone?" suggested Mike, finishing his burger. "Have an-other drink. ...Have lots."

"Can I get naked, too?"

"...Shit, I don't care! Take off your skin if you want."

Carson laughed. "Then I'd really have a boner."

"Oh funny," said Mike.

Carson unbuckled his gun belt and peeled out of his cut-offs. Since his belly hung over his crotch, he didn't look any more naked, at least from a frontal view. "Gots a cam, thug? We can jack-off, make a vid an' get paid. I gots a PayPal account."

"No! ...And quit talking ghetto, it sounds retarded, even when black people do it."

"What's ghetto about a PayPal account?"

"Just chill out, okay?"

"But you got me hard." Carson hoisted his belly with both hands, revealing an un-sunned puffball of fat squeezed between his thighs, from which only the tip of his pink shaft protruded.

Despite himself, Mike asked, "How do you do it?"

"I gots ways. Wanna see?"

"No! ...And being your age got you hard, not me. It's puppy-on-a-curtain stuff... along with nothing Active to do."

"Works for me," said Carson, holding his belly with one hand and using a finger and thumb of the other to manipulate himself. "An' I'd call this active."

"I'd call it desperate," said Mike, "and stop that. ...And you're not gonna bone much unless you lose weight."

"Yeah? How much have you boned with yours?"

Mike got up and went to the window... not that there was much to see.

Carson blew smoke and looked around. "You didn't do much un-packin'."

"I laid down to take a nap."

"Nah, you laid down to dream about me. That's why you was jackin'-off."

Disturbingly true though it was -- partially, at least -- Mike snapped, "I sure as hell wasn't!"

"Give it time an' you will."

"Oh, shut the fuck up!"

"That sounds pretty ghetto."

"Goddammit...!"

"Hey, cool gun!" Carson went over and picked up the shotgun, broke it open expertly to see if it was loaded, then snapped it shut and sighted himself in the cloudy mirror. "This'll knock you on your ass. But whoever you shoot won't get up again."

"Bert Walker gave it to me," said Mike.

"He's nice," said Carson. "Tells me stories."

"He told me about the train robbery in 1897."

"The gold's still out there," said Carson. Then he lowered his voice. "But it's in an Indian burial ground."

"...Did Little Coyote tell you that?"

"Yeah, he knows all about it."

Mike cocked his head. "You saying he knows where it is?"

"Felt my lips move when I said it."

"...So... he could be rich any time he wanted?"

Carson gave Mike an incredulous look. "What about 'Indian burial ground' don't you understand?"

"...Oh," said Mike.

Carson put the gun on the bench and knelt to open a box. "Hey, cool train!" He took out the locomotive. "I seen this kind in a pitcher at the Rattlesnake Saloon."

"It's an Eclipse 0-6-0," said Mike. "There's a picture in the living room. I think it's the same kind of engine they had on the Codyville train. ...They let you in the saloon?"

"Sometimes I have a beer with mom after closin' time."

"That's cool," said Mike. "I have a beer with my dad sometimes."

"He sounds pretty cool," said Carson. "Even if he's broke."

Mike frowned. "Writing is real work, and he works really hard."

"Too bad it don't pay shit."

"Got that right."

"Can I help set up your train?"

"...I don't know if I'm gonna."

"Why not? It's way cool."

"I'd have to build a new layout board. ...And it takes a lot of time."

"Ain't it time you like takin'?"

"...Yeah... but..."

"Get wise to yourself," said Carson. "Lose them dumb-ass dumb-bells, dork, 'cause *they're* what's wastin' your time."

"I'll... take that under advisement," said Mike.

"Wanna come over an' swim in my pool?"

Mike thought that was the best idea he'd heard since coming to Coyote Valley.

"We can get drunk," added Carson, picking up the bottle. "An' post dirty pics an' get paid."

"Can't you just be normal?" asked Mike.

"Okay, we'll just get drunk."

"...I could leave a note for dad... but he should have come back by now."

"With beer?"

"I hope."

"Sounds like you're gettin' desperate."

"Maybe I am, but not for you." Mike heard a snickering sound, but it hadn't been Carson. He leaned out the window... had that been a shadow slipping around the back of the house? "Do you have a dog?"

"No. Why?"

The phone rang in the living room, an old-fashioned bell that took a moment to recognize. Mike padded to answer it with Carson at his heels. He took the receiver off its hook and blew away the dust.

"Hello? Hi, dad, what's up? ...Oh. That sucks. ...That's cool, don't worry about me. I can get something to eat at the store. And some matches to light the lanterns. ...No, the power's not on yet. ...'Course I'm not scared." Mike laughed. "But I won't read one of your books tonight. ...Okay, see you tomorrow. Bye."

"Whatup, dawg?" asked Carson.

"Dammit I told you..."

"Sorry, my bad."

"That was my dad."

"Duh, I gots ears."

"The Land Rover blew a head gasket."

"Told ya Jeeps are better."

"Shut up. The garage in town ordered a new one. It's coming by UPS tomorrow, so he's staying at the hotel."

Carson took another drink. "Maybe he'll go to the Rattlesnake, it's next to the Silver Stallion Hotel."

"I hope not," said Mike.

"Hey, my mom is nice!"

"...Well... probably in her own way."

"She's the best mom in the whole damn world!" Carson clench-ed his fists. "If you say she ain't, I'll kick your ass!"

Mike studied Carson, who, despite his sloppy shape, had taken a fierce fighting stance. "You love her, don't you?"

"'Course I do, you dumb-ass dork!"

Mike ruffled Carson's hair. "That's cool."

"I'll sleep over so you don't get scared."

"There's no power, remember?" said Mike. "We can't play games or go online."

Carson cuddled up to Mike, more comically than anything else. "We can at my crib, homey."

SEVEN

The temperature had lessened a little after the sun had set, though the air was still like a dragon's breath and heat radiated up from the ground. The stars were unbelievably bright, like diamonds gleaming on ebony velvet, as Mike rolled up to his house. He was wearing only the cut-offs he'd made, still wet and cool from swimming, along with his ubiquitous cap. He'd also rigged a sling for the gun out of an old leather belt, and carried the weapon over a shoulder. Carson had advised him to shoot it so he'd know what to expect. He'd braced himself and fired it once out across the desert... and didn't want to shoot it again! His shoulder still ached from the kick.

Even though Carson could drink like a fish he *was* only twelve and had fallen asleep on his air raft adrift in the star-sparkled pool. For the first time since Mike had met him the kid looked youthfully innocent -- or at least unarmed -- and Mike had carried him in to bed, laying him down on a none-too-clean sheet with more than a few suggestive stains. He had dithered a minute before removing Car-son's cut-offs, but he'd read it wasn't healthy to sleep in anything wet, and besides he'd already seen the kid naked, so had gently disrobed him and tucked a blanket up to his chin.

Carson's room, though a nuclear mess and reeking of Carson in every way, was stuffed with the latest electronic toys, including a fifty-inch TV and a super-expensive computer that could have powered the *Enterprise*. There was a Wi with a million games, though not all of them violent or dirty, and a *Thomas The Tank Engine* DVD among the many M-rated films. Mike hadn't intended to snoop, but the air-conditioning made him linger. The rest of the home was fairly well-kept, no worse than his dad's idea of clean, best described as comfortable clutter; and there were cool pictures on the walls: dogs playing poker (his dad had one... which his mother had hated) cute puppies and kittens with huge sad eyes, and a semi-truck with LED lights upon a black velvet background. Surprisingly, there was a book shelf, though mostly ancient paperbacks by Zane Grey, Louis L'amour and other pulp novel authors who'd romanticized the old wild west, where bad guys always wore black hats and tough saloon girls married the hero after the final showdown... obviously Carson's mom's library. The fridge was full of junkfood, which was no surprise -- though the Gansitos were tempting -- and it looked like most of Carson's meals were empty-caloried microwave crap.

There were also many photos of Carson actually looking cute, though seldom in more than cut-offs and gun... unless you counted diapers. He'd been a chubby baby, and his progression to out-of-shape gamer was well documented in time-lapse. His mom was a pretty blond woman in her middle-thirties, who made Mike *think* of tough saloon girls who married the hero in the last scene. But, despite how she made a living, she obviously loved her son. Mike had studied her photos, mostly taken with Carson, and searched her face for evil... though not sure what it would look like. His dad might have gone to the Rattlesnake, but he was too smart to get tricked... Mike hoped. And, except for being a man – a *real* man, and a damn good one -- he didn't have much to get tricked for.

After leaving Carson's cool oasis, Mike had ridden to the store, carefully over the rutted road with only the light of the stars. Snakes sure did come out at night, and he'd been rattled at several times. There wasn't a scarier sound in the world than a rattlesnake's rattle in darkness!

He'd arrived at the store about nine o'clock and bought some miner's candles, a box of wooden matches, a microwave double-cheeseburger and a quart of normal milk, which had taken the last of his cash. He'd eaten his supper out front of the store as the elderly couple who ran the place, Mr. and Mrs. Griswold, were closing for the night; and a black boy toting a shotgun hadn't seemed to scare them. In fact, Mrs. Griswold had smiled and said they carried ten-gauge shells.

Riding back and watching for snakes, he thought he'd glimpsed a dog-like shadow pacing him along the road... but there were lots of shadows out among the cactus. It might have been a coyote, but he wasn't afraid of them anymore after what Bert Walker had said.

He'd almost stopped at Little Coyote's. The ramshackle house looked inviting, its windows glowing with friendly light. But there was a dusty old pickup in front -- a 4X4 International from the 1970s, a toy beside the huge dump truck -- so Little Coyote's sister was home and, judging from the tempting aromas, busy cooking dinner. Mike didn't want to invite himself, though he felt he would have been welcome.

He now leaned his bike against the porch and scanned the nighted desert. As his dad and Bert Walker had said, a gentle breeze had come up after sunset, whispering through the sagebrush, and the windmill was turning slowly with a rhythmic squeaky sound... he'd climb up and oil it tomorrow. But except for that, there was nothing but silence. The sky was ablaze with diamond stars: he'd never known there were so many. The only lights, it seemed, on earth were Little Coyote's windows. Mike suddenly felt very small.

Though it was a little cooler, Mike was panting from the ride. He paused on the porch to light a candle, then padded into his room. He set the candle on the dynamite box after dripping some wax to hold it in place, and lay the gun on his bench. He checked the rusty lantern, but found there was no kerosene... he should have bought a gallon of that instead of the burger and milk. Beginning with his truck stop breakfast of sausage, eggs and hash brown potatoes, he'd already eaten three times as much as he normally ate in a day. If he didn't stay in control of himself, he'd revert to the chubby train-loving boy time-trapped in a frame in his great-uncle's room.

Had he really liked himself then? Or maybe he just hadn't cared how he looked? ...Or maybe not cared if others had cared?

His cut-offs were soaked with sweat -- no surprise -- so he peeled them off and sat down on the bed.

Despite the faint squeak of the windmill, the desert silence was total, and again his breathing seemed too loud. As he had that afternoon, he held his breath and listened, but the echo panting stopped with his own. ...Sure it had. He remembered something his father had said; that "naked" had once meant unprotected, vulnerable... and alone.

And, he couldn't help thinking, even if Little Coyote had said his great-uncle wasn't haunting the house, he *had* passed away in that old brass bed right across the hall. For a moment he thought of closing the door, but that seemed like admitting there *might* be something; and a door wouldn't stop a ghost. Besides, Uncle Joe had apparently liked him, even out of shape.

He supposed he should make up his bed, but who needed blankets in this heat... though he'd heard it got cooler just before dawn. And, though he was still slightly buzzed from the rum, he wasn't tired or sleepy... and tomorrow seemed a light-year away.

Scents of the desert wafted in through the open window. There seemed to be so many at night when during the day there were almost none. There was something that smelled like sex -- at least the only kind he knew -- which kept him sensually half aroused so every movement stirred him. He glanced at his bench, but found he didn't feel guilty at missing two days of pumping iron. He thought about unpacking his train and setting up an oval track, but there was no power to run it. He considered having a session -- he certainly seemed to have plenty of time and his shaft was obviously eager -- but there wasn't any water to wash, and using a sock was never as good.

He went to the window and stood gazing out, while fingertips of sultry breeze caressed his gleaming body. Little Coyote's window glowed, but it was only about ten o'clock... if that kind of time even mattered out here. Mike could just see the dude's rolly shape working on his ship at the table. A boy of the desert who loved ships. Did he ever get lonely, Mike wondered?

A coyote yipped not far away, sounding like crazy laughter. Picking up the candle, Mike went into the living room. Again, his foot-steps seemed eerily echoed, but there was nothing following him... he spun around twice to make sure. After searching several boxes, he found his dad's binoculars... U.S. Navy surplus and huge. Returning to his room, he aimed the glasses into the night, and almost jumped back in surprise... it was like he was at Little Coyote's window.

The desert air was crystal clear; it was if the dude was ten feet away. He seemed to have taken a shower somehow -- maybe under his water tank -- his mammoth body gleaming like his sister's copper pots, and was leaning forward in concentration, the balloons of his breasts spilling onto the table, painting some detail on his ship with an almost microscopic brush, his face concealed by his raven mane. Mike saw a box of Gansitos and a quart of milk, and imagined the radio playing rock.

Then he felt shocked at what he was doing. A girl would have been okay to peep, but not another boy! Was he getting as horny as Carson with nothing Active to do? He threw the binoculars onto the bed. Maybe he should sweep the house? Be a useful engine. Shit! He'd been here less than a day and now he was peeping boys! What would he be doing tomorrow, jacking-off with Carson for perverted pedos with PayPal accounts?

"Stop it!" he yelled to the silence.

Then he held his breath... Little Coyote might have heard. The night was so still and their windows open. He grabbed the glasses and looked again: the dude was still at work. But maybe his radio was on.

"Chill out," said Mike. "You're a little buzzed and lonely with no TV and nothing to do. It's totally *normal* to feel like this. ...At least I guess it is." He paced the little room like a cage, kicking boxes out of his way and raising puffs of dust. He wished he had more alcohol so he could drink and be nothing all night.

"...Well," he finally muttered. "He said to come over, didn't he?" Then he looked in the mirror. "Check me out, I'm talking to myself!" He made a crazy laugh that sounded like a coyote.

His last clean jeans were from back in the day when his waist had been wider than his chest, and now barely clung to his hips. After donning his sneaks, he slung the shotgun over a shoulder, went out the front door and mounted his bike. Again, he thought he saw a shadow vanishing around the house... but maybe the coyotes were checking him out because he'd made their crazy sound?

The air had cooled a little more, which wasn't very much. The stars shone bright as laser points as he slowly navigated the road, and the scent of "sex" was savagely strong. Mike supposed it was some kind of plant; but combined with the sweat-slicked heat in his jeans and the rhythmic friction of pedaling, he couldn't subdue that part of himself. "More than four hours," he muttered.

A coyote laughed not far away.

EIGHT

Fearing he might have an "accident," he finally brought his bike to a stop close to Little Coyote's house. The truck looked even bigger at night, dwarfing the dusty pickup and scenting the air with diesel fuel, engine oil and rusty iron... a sort of mechanical sweat. A light was on in the living room, and there were TV sounds, but it seemed stupid to go to the door since Little Coyote was at his window. Mike walked his bike the rest of the way while tugging at his slipping jeans, which slipped even more from the sweat of his ride: at least they were loose enough to conceal what might have been misunderstood.

A bulb shone over the table; one of those bright unfrosted kind beneath a tin shade like a Chinese hat. Its glare would make it hard to see out, and Little Coyote was intent on his work, pausing only to eat a Gansito -- there was a box of a dozen packs -- or drink from the carton of milk. Mike stopped a few feet away. He hadn't had a Gansito since he'd started eating healthy, but suddenly wanted one now. The radio was bumping low, playing an old Gorillaz song... *remember that it's all in your head.*

"Hi," said Mike.

Little Coyote looked up and smiled from under his tangle of hair. "Heya."

"Hope I didn't scare you," said Mike.

"I'm an Indian, remember? I heard you before you were halfway here, and so did Brother Coyote."

Mike looked around. "There's a coyote out here with me?"

"Did you see one?"

56

"I saw a shadow."

"That's what you can expect to see when Brother Coyote follows you, and he's only letting you see that."

"You know him?" asked Mike.

Little Coyote shrugged. "I know a lot of coyotes."

Mike leaned his bike against the wall. "It's not too late, is it?"

"Nah. Night is when all the cool stuff happens. Sometimes I go out and howl."

"I think I can relate," said Mike.

"Cool coach gun," said Little Coyote. "Guess you shot it around sundown?"

"Yeah," said Mike. "But I don't think I wanna shoot it again. Bert Walker gave it to me. Said it was the gun they carried on the Cody-ville train. He told me about the robbery." Then Mike hesitated, not sure if it was cool to reveal what Carson had told him about the gold in an Indian burial ground.

"Check the ship now," said Little Coyote.

"It rocks," said Mike, leaning in through the window.

"Have a cool swim with Carson?"

"He's basically okay when he's not trying to be a porn star. He got drunk and passed out, so I put him to bed."

"He's not going to say you molested him, but he might be pissed he missed it."

"...I didn't!"

"You're actually going to dignify that?"

"...Oh."

"He needs a good man in his life. He's ready for his passing rite... when a boy becomes a man... but there's no man to show him the way, so he's pretty confused."

"You mean like a ceremony?" asked Mike.

"Ceremonies are good because they honor the time of transition. But they're not really necessary as long as a boy has a man to guide him."

"There's you," said Mike.

"I take him camping a lot, but I can't share many adventures with him in the physical world. That's important, too."

"I'd call camping an adventure."

"But he needs to find his vision quest."

"What about a spirit guide?"

"You know about those?"

"I read books, too," said Mike. "Guides are usually animals, aren't they?"

"Yeah, though they can be other things... birds, reptiles, ele-ments. Most boys have to search for one, usually on the spiritual plane, though sometimes a spirit guide will appear if a boy deserves one."

"Is that how you got yours?"

"How do you know I have one?"

"'Cause you obviously deserve one. ...And I think he's been checking me out all day."

"Brother Coyote loves to play jokes. 'Specially on people who take themselves too seriously."

"Guess I'm one of those," said Mike. "Even my dad said to lighten up."

"Sounds like he's a good man."

"He is," said Mike. "So, you go camping?"

"The old copper mine is a cool place for camping. There's a bunk-house, and a stove for cooking... another one of my hobbies."

"You don't sleep on the ground or cook on a fire?"

Little Coyote kicked back in the chair and patted his gigantic belly, making it ripple like ocean waves. "Life is already full of things that are hard, dirty, and painful, you don't have to make up your own."

"I kinda been doing that," said Mike.

"Yeah, it shows." Little Coyote smiled. "You can come with us and sleep on the ground if you think that's building your model Mike."

"I think I'd like the bunkhouse better. ...I guess the logical question is, what am I trying to build? ...Or who?"

"Two good questions," said Little Coyote.

"Do spirit guides help with stuff like that?"

"One of their primary functions. ...Want to come in? I'll snag us some beers."

"Should I go to the door?"

"Climb in the window. My sister's probably going to bed."

Mike started to mount the window sill. "Ow! ...Something bit my leg! ...Maybe it's a rattlesnake!"

"Is it still holding on?" asked Little Coyote, who didn't look very concerned.

"Yeah! It's got me bad!"

"That's jumping cactus," said Little Coyote. "The spines are so sharp you can't feel 'em go in till they stick your jeans to your skin. A rattlesnake bites and then lets go to see if he needs to bite again. C'mon, climb in and I'll pull 'em out."

Mike hoisted himself over the sill, dragging his wounded leg and almost losing his jeans. He heard a coyote's laughter.

Little Coyote smiled again. "Warned you, didn't I?"

"The desert doesn't like people, does it? Everything's got spikes or bites!"

"Cactus has spines so it doesn't get eaten or have its stored water sucked out. And most things bite to defend themselves. ...Sit on the bed and stretch out your leg."

"Ow!" yelped Mike, sitting down. "Is it bad?"

Little Coyote searched his table, found a pair of needle-nose pliers, and ponderously knelt to study Mike's leg. "You only got six or seven. ...This won't hurt much. They come out as easy as they go in."

"Shit!" said Mike. "What if I fell off my bike into one?"

"You have to learn to live *with* the desert. Only a fool just tries to live in it. Respect it, and pay attention to what it's telling you. And become a part of it. Become a coyote, a rattlesnake, a lizard or a bird. The cactus didn't attack you, you invaded its space." Little Coyote got busy. "Don't wiggle or you'll break 'em off. ...See, they come out easy," he added, displaying a six-inch spine.

"That's cool... I guess," said Mike. "...Um... what's that smell in the air?"

"Another kind of cactus. It always smells like sex at night. And that's when most of it goes on."

"That's gonna take getting used to."

"I noticed," said Little Coyote. "You were radiating until you got stuck."

"...Radiating what?"

59

"Nothing to be ashamed of. According to nature you're ready to mate, therefore you're advertising."

"...Oh." Mike studied Little Coyote's enormous avalanche of belly. "...Um... Logical progression of thought?"

Little Coyote laughed. "It's jacking-off, Jim, but not as you know it." He pulled out the last of the spines, got laboriously to his feet and tossed them out the window. "I didn't see your dad come back."

Mike explained what had happened.

"That sucks," said Little Coyote. "Being alone your first night here. Brother Coyote might have had fun with you."

"I think he already did," said Mike, rubbing his leg, though it didn't hurt much.

"Had supper?"

"A microwave burger and milk."

"My sister made Navajo tacos... fry-bread, ground beef and a lot of good stuff. There's still a few warm on the stove."

"Thanks," said Mike. "I thought you were Apache?"

"Traditional Apache food is mostly kill something and eat it." Little Coyote pointed to the old Yellow Boy. "*This* fat kid can hunt if he has to, but it's easier to score at the store."

"Isn't using a gun kinda cheating?"

"Then so is using a spear. Or a bow and arrow. ...Can you press 200 pounds?"

"Sure," said Mike, flexing an arm.

"Do fifty pushups?"

"One handed."

"But, can you run down a rabbit? Or kill a deer with your teeth?"

"'Course not."

"Neither could our ancestors no matter how 'in shape' they were. That's why the Great Spirit gave us brains; not only so we could just survive but also have the consciousness to know there's something more to life than just surviving long enough to reproduce our species."

"Food for thought," said Mike, then asked, "Um, do you really talk like that? 'Great Spirit' and that kinda stuff?"

"No, but you don't speak Apache, in which those words don't

sound like dialog written by white-eyes for old western movies."

About a half hour later, Mike was kicked back on the bed, his belly stuffed with delicious food and round despite the muscles. He sipped from a bottle of cold San Miguel, which didn't go bad with Gansitos. "If lard is the devil, take me to hell."

Little Coyote was at the table cleaning his tiny brushes. "You sleepy?" he asked.

"Not really." Mike ate another Gansito. "Maybe I'm getting used the desert where everything happens at night."

"Want to take a cruise in my truck?"

"Yeah. Cool."

The living room was dark now, but a female voice called from the hall as Mike, toting his shotgun, and Little Coyote with his rifle, started out the front door: "Little Coyote?"

"Nah, it's a Little Gray from Area 51. I'm going for a drive with Mike, the dude who moved in up the road."

"Watch out for snakes."

"Everybody says that," said Mike.

"She meant about running 'em over. That's bad medicine."

Mike laughed. "In my case bad ju-ju."

NINE

The air was almost comfortable now as Mike followed Little Coyote to the mammoth truck beneath the stars. It felt good to be shirtless out in the night; sort of wild and free. A coyote howled and he answered it, surprised when it answered back. "What did he say?"

"Not bad, but you sound hyena."

"No surprise," said Mike.

Little Coyote went to the truck, climbed ponderously onto the running-board and opened the cab's rusty door. Then Mike saw a four-legged shape emerge from under the vehicle.

"Thought you didn't have a dog."

"I don't," said Little Coyote.

"...So... I guess that's a coyote?" asked Mike, drawing back a little as the animal came up to him, but wasn't wagging its tail. Its scent was mostly sagebrush, its eyes amber-bright in the pale moon glow.

"Don't look like a hyena. Or would that be an hyena?"

"I don't know ...Um, should I pet him?"

"He might want flowers and candy first."

Mike offered a hand to be sniffed, then gently stroked the coyote's head. "What's his name?"

"We haven't met, but if he likes you he'll tell you."

"Is he gonna come with us?"

"Guess that's why he's here." Little Coyote held the door open and the coyote bounded into the cab.

Mike went around to the passenger door while Little Coyote maneuvered his bulk behind the massive steering wheel, his belly squeezed tightly underneath, the balloons of his breasts lolling over the rim. The seat was ancient leather, and the coyote sat in the middle, its fur much coarser than a dog's, its scent a lot more wild.

Little Coyote a pulled a handle, "Compression release." He pushed a button and the engine started, shaking the massive vehicle and sounding like mechanical thunder.

"Tops out at 35," Little Coyote said, as they rumbled away from the house.

"Who needs to go faster?" said Mike, kicking back with an arm out the window, the coyote's panting breaths in one ear, hot and smelling carnivorous... not unlike his own. Mike looked around at the moonlit desert and distant mountains under the stars. "How far can we go?"

"Not all the way on a first date."

"Does Carson write your material?"

"We could go to the old copper mine." Little Coyote smiled at their furry companion. "The brothers hang out there a lot. Just don't be too serious."

"I'll laugh at their jokes."

"Just be yourself, they see though posers."

"Ever been to the ghost town?"

"Codyville? Nope. Only way there is the old railroad track, and it's narrow-gauge so this truck can't fit. And I'm way too fat to hike that far."

"Are the rails still there?" asked Mike.

"What you can see going up the mountains, and there's a spur to the copper mine. They used to haul ore into Coyote Flats when the Santa Fe still connected."

Mike thought for a moment. "If there's still track to Codyville, maybe we could build something to run on it? ...Like a little rail car, if we had a motor."

"I like your mind," said Little Coyote. "There's a lot of junk at the mine; tons of old machinery, and truck parts in the shop. And one-cylinder engines they used to power water pumps. Probably mine carts in the old shafts... they were narrow-gauge, too. We could bolt an engine to one of those and rig a chain drive to the wheels."

"We have tools," said Mike.

"And opposable thumbs."

"So, you wanna build a rail car and go to Codyville? ...Like, one of those old-time stories for boys nobody writes anymore."

"That would be cool." Little Coyote smiled in the yellow glow of the dashboard lights. "But, I'd think you'd want to look for the gold instead of exploring a ghost town."

The coyote cocked its head at Mike, who said, "Bert Walker told me the story about the wagon disappearing and nobody ever finding it. ...But, Carson said..."

"The gold's in an Indian burial ground?" Little Coyote laughed. "I made that up so he wouldn't go looking and get in trouble out there. He knows the desert pretty well, but he doesn't always pay atten-tion."

"So, you don't know where the gold is?"

Little Coyote laughed again as they rumbled past Mike's house. "I live in a shack in the desert, and we're not rolling a Maserati... assuming I could fit in one." He guided the truck around a snake winding its way across the road. "And if my people had gotten the gold, we'd own this valley today. Probably have a casino resort and an 'authentic village' for tourists with a restaurant serving buffalo burgers."

"I didn't think there were buffaloes here; weren't they in the Great Plains?"

"Hey, you are smart."

"What about a steam railroad? ...Like, reactivate the Codyville line?"

"Not a 'health and fitness' camp?"

The coyote seemed to snicker."

"Hey, c'mon," said Mike.

"Not ethnic, but a good money-maker."

"A Native-American railroad," said Mike. "The only one in this country."

"Works for me," said Little Coyote, "assuming we had the gold."

"Have you ever looked for it?"

"Your uncle took me with him sometimes until I was about eleven and got too fat to get on a mule, so I know lots of places it's not." Little Coyote made a detour around another snake. "The robbers only had five hours to make a getaway." He pointed north-east. "The land is rough and rocky out there. An ore wagon with a four horse team could make about three miles an hour over level ground, but there it could barely go one."

"A five mile radius," said Mike. "From where they robbed the train."

"Less than that," said Little Coyote. "Coyote Flats is south, so they wouldn't have gone that way. West is open country, so they would have been easy to spot. The copper mine is north, so the miners would have seen them."

"So they must have gone east," said Mike.

"Seems like the only choice they had, but it wouldn't have made any sense 'cause they couldn't have gotten over the mountains. Only reason they *might* have gone east is all the old mines out there... roll in the wagon, blow up the entrance, and ride away on the horses. That's what your great-uncle thought."

"What about the wheel tracks? Bert Walker said there weren't any."

"Like I said, the ground is rocky. And the government had run us out, so the sheriff didn't have Indian trackers."

"That would narrow the field a lot." Mike spread a hand toward the eastern mountains. "Like a fan from where the robbery hap-pened. No more than five miles long or wide."

"Even less," said Little Coyote, avoiding another snake. "It's only a mile from the robbery site to the feet of those mountains, so the fan is only a mile long."

"That's not a very big area," said Mike. "Seems like it would be easy to search."

"You haven't seen the land out there. It's cut all over by gulches and washes. Can't even drive a jeep very far. That's why your great-uncle had mules."

Mike glanced at the furry coyote, who'd pricked up his ears at the mention of gold. "Wouldn't they know where it is?"

"I'm sure they do."

"Logical progression of thought...?"

"Ask him," Little Coyote suggested.

"...But, can't you talk to them?"

"Only when they want to talk."

TEN

Mike pointed ahead. "The lights are on at Carson's. When does his mom come home?"

"Usually not for a few more hours," Little Coyote replied. "Want to take him with us?"

"He's gotta be a little lonely, even with 200 channels."

"He could use some healthy fun."

"Or the normal kind," said Mike.

"He's probably heard us by now anyway."

"Yeah, here he comes," said Mike, as Carson ran out on the porch clad in his cut-offs and cannon again.

Little Coyote swung the truck into the mobile home's front yard, halting with a hiss of brakes. Carson leaped down the steps and came running.

"Wait for me!" he shouted like anyone's little brother. He was almost past the swimming pool when he suddenly cursed and fell in the dirt. "Snake!" he squalled, clutching his foot. "Fuckin' little bastard!"

"Oh shit!" cried Mike.

"Stay cool," said Little Coyote and avalanched out of the cab, thudding massively to the ground and raising a billow of dust. "There's a knife in the glove box."

He moved a lot faster than Mike would have thought, lumbering over to Carson in the glow of the truck's headlights. Mike found the knife and scrambled out, the coyote close behind.

"Watch it, Mike! There goes the snake! Don't get in his way!" Little Coyote plopped down beside Carson, who was yelling every dirty

66

word Mike had ever heard... along with a few he hadn't.

"Oh, shut up!" Little Coyote snapped. "You weren't paying attention again! ...Where'd he get you?"

"On my big toe, goddamn it to hell!"

"Should I call 911?" asked Mike.

Little Coyote checked Carson's foot. "We don't have a 911. Doc Millburn's number is in the book, but it'll take him half an hour. Give me the knife and go call."

"What's the address here?"

"Miss Kitty's place."

A few minutes later, Mike ran back in the hot desert night. He'd only seen people get snake-bit in movies, and figured it was serious shit, but Carson was looking smart-ass while Little Coyote sucked his toe and spit bright blood in the headlight beams. The furry coyote sat nearby, watching with its bright amber eyes.

"The doctor's on his way," panted Mike. "Is Carson gonna be all right?"

Little Coyote spit more blood. "The snake didn't get him very bad, only grazed him with a fang. Carry him inside and put him on the couch."

Mike gathered Carson up in his arms.

"My big strong hero," Carson sighed, giving Mike a kiss on the cheek.

"Shut up!" snapped Mike.

The coyote gave a yipping laugh, and Little Coyote got to his feet. "I'll get some ice, that'll slow down the swelling. Prop him up with pillows so his foot's way down below his heart."

"Does it hurt?" asked Mike, after arranging Carson on a purple velvet sofa with heart-shaped crimson pillows. The coyote had followed them in and was sitting calmly watching below the poker-playing dogs.

Carson winced a little... his toe was beginning to swell. But then he made kissy lips. "Not as much as my heart for you."

"Stop that shit," said Mike.

"Be nice to me, I might be dyin'. Maybe you should suck it some more?"

"Should I?" asked Mike, as Little Coyote came in from the kitchen with ice cubes in a dishcloth.

"Good idea."

Mike knelt down and took Carson's foot, its sole as tough as leather.

"Too bad it ain't my dick," snarked Carson.

The coyote laughed again.

"That's not funny!" snapped Mike, turning to the coyote.

Carson cocked his head. "Who you talkin' to?"

"The coyote, duh."

"What coyote?" asked Carson, looking around.

Mike turned to the laughing coyote again, then looked up at Little Coyote. "...Um, is that your spirit guide?"

Little Coyote smiled. "No, but I think he's yours."

ELEVEN

Mike woke up to the scent of a coyote, wild and earthy, a part of the desert. Actually, he scented two coyotes because he'd been sleeping on the floor of Little Coyote's den, and the dude also smelled like a part of the desert.

The furry coyote lay curled beside Mike on a single Indian blanket, which wasn't much of a mattress. Still, Mike had slept peace-fully, though that probably wasn't surprising considering all the physical stuff he'd done the day before -- toting he and his dad's possessions into his great-uncle's house, climbing up to unlock the windmill, riding sweaty miles on his bike -- until, a little past mid-night, they'd returned here in the Euclid with Mike's new brother riding shotgun.

After the doctor had left in a battered Dodge 4X4 ambulance, taking Carson to his home in town -- which was also a medical clinic as well as a funeral parlor -- Little Coyote suggested that Mike spend the night with him... an invitation he'd gladly accepted.

Mike had also accepted, after the doctor arrived -- another wild-west character like the crusty old Doc in *Gunsmoke* -- and given Carson a shot of rattlesnake anti-venom, only Mike and Little Coyote could see Mike's furry brother. Nevertheless, it seemed strange that though the coyote was spiritual, it could feel and smell so real... its coarse fur brushing his shoulder, its carnivore breath hot on his cheek as they'd driven back in the truck.

Lying here now on the blanket, barefoot in only his jeans, Mike again felt an actual coyote beside him and remembered asking its name as they'd bedded down for the night. It had made a gruffy sound, which of course Mike couldn't pronounce. Then Mike had heard a voice in his mind: *Ruff will suffice in your tongue.*

Mike had turned to Little Coyote, who had shed his jeans and sneaks and was settling into bed. "Did you hear that?"

Little Coyote had laughed. "Duh will suffice in our tongue."

Now, Ruff woke up -- why would a spirit need to sleep? -- gave Mike a sly look, then bounded out through the open window. *Later, bro,* said the voice in Mike's mind.

Mike sat up. "When?" he called.

"Hopefully when you need him," Little Coyote said, rolling ponderously onto his side and brushing the hair away from his eyes.

"Hopefully?"

"I warned you about Brother Coyote. He has a kind heart but loves to play jokes."

Mike yawned and stretched. The morning air was relatively cool, but there was a feeling of oncoming heat, like a huge thermal wave on the horizon rolling inexorably in. "Do people get the guides they need?"

"They get the guides they deserve." Little Coyote laughed. "Mine's also a coyote."

"Will I get to meet him?"

"That's pretty rare, seeing someone's else's guide. Yours only let me see him 'cause you weren't ready to meet him alone."

"Yeah, that would have freaked me. ...Who chooses your guide? The Great Spirit? ... Since I don't speak Apache."

"Your guide chooses you."

Mike got to his feet and tugged up his jeans. "What kind of guide will Carson get?"

"A crow might be appropriate, being notorious smart-asses, but your guess is as good as mine."

"I hope he's okay."

"The snake only wanted to teach him a lesson." Little Coyote also got up, all his rolls rearranging themselves to conform with the law of gravity and his vast belly plunging down to his knees.

"Does his mom know what happened?"

"The whole town probably knows by now."

A female voice called from the kitchen, "Breakfast is ready."

"On our way," Little Coyote replied.

Mike had logically assumed that Little Coyote's sister would also be super-size, but she was merely "pleasingly plump," a term he probably wouldn't have used twenty-four hours ago. She was maybe nineteen with large dark eyes in a chubby-cheeked face and rosebud lips that easily smiled, her raven hair bound in a ponytail that flowed midway down her back, her lush figure clad in a white cotton dress appropriate for a lady chef. She wore a necklace of turquoise beads, and a bracelet of silver and onyx.

The tantalizing aromas of breakfast made lustful love to Mike's nose as he trailed Little Coyote into the kitchen. The table, with red and white checkered cloth, transported him back to -- yes, he admitted – a happier time when eating food that tasted good with-out calculating calories had been an innocent pleasure instead of a guilt-provoking sin. There were the big colorful plates, tumblers of milk and orange juice, and silverware with Bakelite handles, circa 1920s.

Little Coyote's sister, whose name was Dancing Fox, had piled the plates with -- surprising Mike -- an enormous "paleface" morning repast of scrambled eggs with melted cheese, plump and juicy sausage links, mountains of crispy golden hash-browns, and thick buttered slabs of whole-wheat toast.

"Try this," Little Coyote suggested, seating himself across from Mike on a very sturdy homemade chair and indicating a Mason jar. "Prickly-pear jelly, one of my sister's specialties."

Mike spread some on his toast, took a bite and his tongue went to heaven. "How long has this been going on?" He turned to Dancing Fox. "Heap-big awesome! ... Since I don't speak Apache."

Dancing Fox dimpled her cheeks. "Thank you." Then she said to Little Coyote, "I have to be going... do wash the dishes."

"Dutifully," Little Coyote replied around a mouthful of sausage and eggs.

Despite all he'd eaten the day before, Mike was as hungry as a starving coyote, and his belly was bulging tight and round after he'd finally cleaned his plate. Though feeling almost too stuffed to move, he helped Little Coyote with the dishes, asking as he dried them, "When do you want to go to the mine and build our rail car?"

Little Coyote hung up a frying pan. "Still want to go to Codyville rather than look for the gold?"

Mike put the plates on a shelf. "Isn't it mostly dreamers who go out looking for gold? And in most of the stories I've read, nothing good ever happens to them even if they find it."

"It's the basic quest theme," said Little Coyote, "shared by cultures all over the world. There's no free lunch in the universe: you have to be worthy to be rewarded; face some danger and over-come hardship to prove your strength. And not just in the physical world; you have to be spiritually in shape."

"My dad said something like that," said Mike. "You think that's why the coyotes never told anyone where it is? No one's been wor-thy to find it?"

"Could be," said Little Coyote, hanging up the last pan. "But they also know that even good people can be corrupted by wealth, and the rich have never been kind to coyotes."

"Who would the gold belong to if somebody did find it?"

Little Coyote cleaned the sink. "Your great-uncle talked about that. The gold mining company went out of business in 1917. The insurance company went bankrupt during the Great Depression in 1933. The gold was out of the ground and refined, so it doesn't belong to the state. So, it's anybody's who finds it."

"What would you do if you found it?"

"See the seven seas. What would you do?"

"...Maybe buy a steam railroad. ...Want any company on your cruise?"

"Welcome aboard."

"Guess that shows we're not worthy," said Mike. "We should have said we'd help poor people... though I would, wouldn't you? I mean with *some* of the money."

"Wealth would be another test." Little Coyote straightened the tablecloth. "We can go to the mine anytime, but it would be cool to take Carson."

"Yeah, it would be good exercise... both ways, I mean." Mike hung up the dish towel. "I should go home in case my dad calls. Come over and I'll show you my train."

"Load your bike in the truck and let's ride."

About ten minutes later, the mammoth Euclid rolled to a stop in front of Mike's house. Little Coyote shut off the engine, and Mike heard the telephone bell. He leaped from the cab and dashed to the house -- though paying attention for snakes as he ran -- and snatched the receiver off its hook.

"Hello?" he puffed. "...Hi, dad. ...I'm fine. ...Oh, you heard about Carson. ...From his mom last night. ...At the Rattlesnake Saloon. ...I guess she's kinda nice... but..."

The front porch creaked, and Little Coyote filled the doorway... at least on the horizontal plane. "She's had a lot of boyfriends," he suggested with a smile.

Mike considered that, but asked his dad instead, "Do you know how Carson is? ...Cool." He turned to Little Coyote, who'd entered toting the guns, the floorboards vocalizing beneath his dusty sneaks. "His mom's bringing him home today. ...Oh, that's Little Coyote, dad. Lives in the house with the awesome dump truck. He's really awesome, too."

"Aw shucks," said Little Coyote.

"...The power?" said Mike.

Little Coyote pulled the string of the bare bulb on a rafter. Nothing happened.

"It's still off," said Mike. "...Yeah, I unlocked it yesterday. ...I'll check the tank. ...Did the gasket come in? ...So, you should be back this afternoon? ...KFC?" Mike grinned at Little Coyote. "Bring a lot. Little Coyote will be here for dinner. ...And beer, San Miguel. ...Okay. Love you, too."

Mike turned to Little Coyote again. "Wish I had some Cokes or beer. And there's nothing to eat."

"We can have lunch at my place. I'll make us more Navajo tacos."

Mike pointed. "That's my room. I'll check the water tank and join you in a minute. ...Sorry it's so hot in here."

"Guess that's why you're sweating," observed Little Coyote, who wasn't.

The breeze had died at dawn, and the windmill now hung motionless as Mike emerged from the house's back door into the rapidly mounting heat. The tank was maybe a quarter full but, as predicted, was leaking. Mike stood under one of the trickles to wash off some of the sweat.

Little Coyote was in Mike's room, regarding the weight bench as if it smelled bad. "Looks like a torture device," he said.

"You can sit there if you want," said Mike. "I don't think the bed would hold you."

But Little Coyote subsided "Indian fashion" onto the floor, his vast middle spreading around him like a blubbery torus. "No thanks, it radiates."

"Radiates what?" asked Mike.

"Call it negative energy, and Ruff pissed on it."

"...Oh," said Mike, though seeing no supernatural puddle. "He's like my personal trainer now? ...To get me in spiritual shape?"

"Good metaphor," said Little Coyote. He leaned the guns against a wall. "You should only have things around you that give you positive energy and celebrate who you are. That thing was draining your energy."

Mike couldn't help posing a bit as the model Mike he'd made. "But, it's made me stronger."

"That isn't the kind of strength you need to face whatever lies ahead."

"You mean my vision quest?"

"The rest of your life is a vision quest."

"Can Ruff see my future?"

"If he could, he wouldn't tell you; that would spoil the fun."

"His or mine?"

"Both of you." Little Coyote indicated a box. "That radiates very positive and celebrates you all over the place."

It was the box containing the train, and Mike knelt to open it. "Guess I've gotten those feelings, too, but I haven't been paying attention to them." He took out the locomotive. "This is the same kind of engine they had on the Codyville train. Like a cool coincidence."

"I've seen the picture," said Little Coyote. "It was taken the day of the robbery by the *Coyote Valley Times*. You can see the boxcar door is open."

"I didn't look that close," said Mike. He handed the engine to Little Coyote, went into the living room and took the picture off the wall. Returning, he sat beside Little Coyote and brushed all the dust off the glass.

"Yeah, it is open. ...And, if you look real close, you can see faces in the engine's cab windows... probably the engineer and the fireman. ...And maybe the brakeman. ...Can't see 'em very well, but they all look kinda young. 'Course, steam was new technology then, and evolving fast like computers today, so a lot of young people were into steam."

"Sounds like you know a lot about steam," said Little Coyote, still checking the engine. "More than just from a model train."

"I bought an old book in a pawn shop: *Catechism Of The Locomotive.*" Mike lay the picture on the floor and went to open another box. He took out a heavy old book bound in ragged black buckram, then sat beside Little Coyote again and leafed though the yellowed pages. "It's got everything about steam locomotives in the 1800s, from how they were built to how to run them."

Little Coyote scanned the book. "It also radiates positive." Then he picked up the picture and compared it to Mike's locomotive. "They have the same number."

Mike looked at the photo again, then at his locomotive: both had the number 22 on a brass plate on the front of their boilers. "Funny, I didn't notice that. Good models are made from factory plans of real locomotives. ...Don't seem like they'd have more than one or two engines on a little railroad, so it's probably a factory number... the twenty-second of the series. Eclipse was a small company, not like Baldwin or some of the others that made locomotives back then, and mostly specialized in switchers. ...But it's kinda... I dunno... spooky! ...Or maybe like some kinda sign."

Little Coyote looked thoughtful. "Not every coincidence is a sign. ...But some are."

TWELVE

"**B**reakfast!" called Mike's dad from the kitchen.

Mike opened his eyes and yawned, lying naked on his bed atop its single blanket. It must have been around nine o'clock, the sun streaming in through the open window and the temperature rapidly rising. Like most boys his age he woke full of life, and usually had a work-out that wasn't pumping metallic iron. But the house was so small, its walls so thin, and the rusty bedsprings squeaked, so, for the last two days, he'd been "working-out" in the patch of shade beneath the water tank. But he'd overslept this morning, after being with Carson -- who was back to his usual smart-ass self -- at Little Coyote's until after midnight, loading the mammoth Euclid for a trip to the copper mine.

"Okay!" he called, getting up, his shaft still jutting joyfully with only one thing on its mono-track mind.

He'd unpacked all his things by now, installed his clothes in the dresser -- after evicting a scorpion -- and built a table and book shelves from the weathered old boards of the outhouse. The power had been restored yesterday, and he, Carson and Little Coyote had set up his train on the floor, then lain on their bellies side-by-side and taken turns being engineer. Mike's games and computer were on the table, and his books now filled the shelves... though *Catechism Of The Locomotive* lay on the bedside dynamite box. Though he didn't know why, he'd found new interest in the old book, and had spent many hours reading it.

His bench and weights were gone. After dinner two nights ago -- a feast of KFC and beer shared with Little Coyote -- he'd carried it all to the outhouse and dumped it down the old shit-hole. He'd heard Ruff laugh as he'd dropped the last dumb-bell: *That's a good start to clearing your track.*

Mike's dad had only looked thoughtful when Mike had returned to the house, and they'd sipped the last pair of San Miguels out on the porch under the stars while Mike told his father about the plan to go to Codyville.

"You're welcome to come," he'd added. "Like, see what you missed when you were thirteen."

His dad had smiled. "Thanks, Mike. But that's something I should have done then, and now my vision would only cloud yours."

"What do you mean?" Mike had asked.

"It's *your* adventure, Mike. Yours, Carson's, and Little Coyote's. There'll probably be some danger, and if I was along I'd warn you about it. And maybe I'd be too careful and you wouldn't do something you should have done. A lot of people today would say that's being a good parent, but that's why a lot of today's kids never be-come self-reliant."

"I think I get that," Mike had said. "Like, I have to make mistakes; learn some things the hard way. ...Is that why you never discouraged me when I got those weights?"

"There are many roads to manhood, Mike, and if you don't explore a few you'll always wonder what you missed. Or what kind of man you might have become if you'd done something different. ...But, make *educated* mistakes based on the knowledge you already have."

"Like, look before you leap?"

"Think before you act. Stop and consider what could go wrong before you take a risk."

"Sounds like something Little Coyote would say."

"Sounds like you found a good friend."

"Carson is pretty cool, too... in a punky little brother way." Then Mike had asked. "Did Uncle Joe tell you about the gold when you were here at my age?"

"He was always out looking for it, and took me with him a few times."

"Those must have been adventures."

"Not very exciting adventures... plodding all day on the back of a mule under the blazing sun. Climbing in and out of gullies. And nothing to see but cactus and rocks. He must have searched every inch of that ground between the railroad tracks and the mountains."

"It can't be a very big area. Little Coyote and me figured that out."

"If you see the land out there you'll know how hard it is to search it. Makes you wonder how a big heavy wagon could have gotten away."

"Maybe they didn't?" Mike had said. "Maybe the robbers wanted the sheriff to *think* they'd gotten away with the gold, but they really hadn't? ...Like, maybe there was a mine shaft close to the railroad tracks? ...Or, maybe they'd dug a big hole near the tracks before they robbed the train? There were four of them, so they might have been able to bury the wagon before the posse got there."

His dad had nodded. "That was one of Uncle Joe's theories, but he had a lot of them... maybe they only buried the *gold?* Which wouldn't have needed a very big hole. And, what if they'd stolen the wagon from the copper mine and driven it back on the railroad bed, which wouldn't have left many traces."

"...Yeah," Mike had said. "And since the wagon was back at the mine, nobody knew they'd used it. ...So, maybe it *is* just the gold that's really buried out there. ...What would you do if you got rich? Would you stop writing?"

"No, because I like writing, Mike. Call it my 'art' if you want to get high-toned. And it's something a writer has to do, no matter if they're rich or poor... like painters paint and singers sing. And money can't make you a better writer."

"What if you were rich enough to start your own publishing company?"

"Sure, I'd publish my own books. Along with a lot of other black books that white publishers won't publish. And adventure stories for boys, which aren't being published much either in a time when boys need them more than ever. And, money can help promote books... buy ads in papers and magazines so people are aware of them. And get distribution to book stores. But, you can't pay people to *like* your books no matter how rich you are."

"Just like you can't buy real friends. ...Would you move us someplace else?"

"I kind of like it here, Mike, though it's probably pretty boring for you."

"Actually, no," Mike had said.

"It's a good place for me to write, son... no cars driving past, no neighbors' lawnmowers or little kids yelling, or somebody calling their dog."

"So, you wouldn't move if we got rich?"

"I'd make some home improvements, including a good air-conditioner." Then his dad had laughed. "Planning to look for the Codyville gold?"

"Everyone says it's still out there."

His dad had said half-seriously, "Beware of gold fever, son. Once you catch it, you've got it forever."

Now, Mike put on his jeans, one of his newer pairs, and found them a little too tight. But, that wasn't surprising since he'd been eating every day like... well, like a normal boy of his age. He regarded himself in the mirror... his six-pack had softened a little, and his pecs showed signs of reverting to roundness. He smiled at the midnight boy in the glass and donned his newsboy cap. "I'm not sure who you are yet, but I think I'm starting to like you again."

The house had been cleaned -- at least to male standards -- and his dad had set up his writing desk at the living room window, while dogs playing poker now hung on a wall. There were golden pan-cakes for breakfast -- one of his dad's specialties -- with scrambled eggs and bacon. To drink there was coffee -- the old-fashioned kind, boiled in a blue enamel pot -- along with OJ and normal milk. The water tank had begun to fill, and the swamp cooler thrummed on the roof, bathing the kitchen with almost cool air. Mike sat down at the table, and his father joined him a moment later, also only clad in jeans.

"When are you leaving?" asked his dad, after taking a sip of coffee.

"After lunch," said Mike, buttering his pancakes and slathering them with syrup. "Little Coyote's making Navajo tacos." He took a bite of pancake. "If we can build a rail car and get to Codyville, we should be back in about three days."

His dad forked scrambled eggs. "If you aren't, I'll form a posse."

Mike ate a slice of bacon. "If we get in trouble we'll make smoke signals... I'm serious, dad. Three columns of smoke mean help. They'll be easy to see up in the mountains."

"Doesn't Carson have a phone? From what his mother told me about him, he seems to have everything else an American boy would want."

"Maybe except what he needs," said Mike around a mouthful of pancake. "But you can't get a signal out here. ...Um, she's had a lot of boyfriends."

"I'm not insentient, son. And you know I haven't been celibate since your mother left."

"Yeah... I mean I guessed that." Then Mike laughed. "Besides, we don't have anything."

His father raised an eyebrow. "Mike."

"...Well... you know what I mean."

"I get the gist. But, you haven't met her, Mike, so maybe you should reserve your judgment."

"...Well, I know she loves Carson, so that's gotta count."

"Who loves me?" Carson demanded, appearing in the doorway. As usual he was "dressed" in only his short cut-off jeans, his punky decorations and enormous watch, his gun belt overlapped by his belly, the gun barrel almost dragging the floor.

"Everybody I know," said Mike. "Sit down and have some breakfast."

Carson looked suspicious. "Is that 'healthy' food?"

"Yeah," said Mike. "'Cause it tastes good and there's plenty of it."

THIRTEEN

As Mike had seen when he'd climbed the windmill, the copper mine looked like a meteor crater, and all the more awesome up close... a gigantic pit in the reddish-brown earth, three-hundred feet deep and a half mile across. A road spiraled up from the bottom, and he could picture trucks like the Euclid toiling along loaded with ore. There must have been steam shovels digging below and making lots of dust and noise, but now there was nothing but hot desert silence as Little Coyote halted his truck at the edge of the pit and shut off its clattering engine.

The boys dismounted, and Mike scanned around as Carson fired a Camel. The pit lay at the rumble-strewn feet of Coyote Valley's eastern mountains, and he could see the old narrow-gauge track switchbacking up to a pass. Carson pointed across the pit to a cluster of red-rusted buildings. "The shop an' all the ol' junk's over there."

"What about a mine cart?" asked Mike. "That seems like the first thing we need."

"There's a few shafts behind those buildings," Little Coyote said. "Most of the vertical shafts were dug up after the mine went open-pit, but the old ones went into the mountains. They were played out by then, and the company didn't need carts anymore so they pro-bably left them inside."

"So, let's go get one!" piped Carson.

The boys climbed back in the truck and rumbled around the pit. Though the mine had been closed for only a year, it looked more like a hundred to Mike, the rusty buildings falling apart with sheets of tin hanging loose, their dark windows staring like empty skull eyes, and

81

sagebrush and tumbleweeds everywhere.

"There's the spur to the Codyville line," Little Coyote said. "The junction's about a half-mile south."

"It looks in fairly good shape," said Mike. "What you can see from here, anyway."

"Here's the shop," said Carson, as they stopped in front of a barn-like building with doors big enough for a Euclid to enter. A junkyard lay to one side of the structure, piled with ancient machinery and the dismantled corpses of several Euclids.

Again, silence settled as the boys dismounted. Little Coyote pointed. "One of the shafts is behind the shop. It was probably the main shaft back in the 1800s, 'cause its rails connect to the spur and it's big enough for a locomotive."

Mike lifted Carson onto his shoulders and boosted him into the truck bed. The gear they had loaded last night included two ice chests of food, six-packs of Coke and San Miguel beer. A dynamite box held pots and pans, tin plates, cups, and silverware. There were Indian blankets to sleep in, two five-gallon Army cans of water, and Mike and Little Coyote's tools. They'd loaded Carson's minibike before leaving Mike's house an hour ago, like a life boat aboard a liner.

Carson vanished into the bed and returned with three kerosene lanterns. Then he handed down three canteens of galvanized steel with blanket-cloth covers. Last came Mike's school pack, which now contained a few basic tools, miner's candles, a first-aid kit, a coil of rope, a six-pack of Coke, and a box of Gansitos. Mike shouldered the pack, then helped Carson down.

"My big strong hero," cooed Carson.

"Stop that shit," said Mike.

Little Coyote had taken Mike's gun and his Yellow Boy out of the cab. "There'll be snakes in the mine; they go in hunting for rats; but don't shoot if you don't have to."

"Can't you talk to them?" asked Mike.

"Sometimes they don't wait for explanations." Little Coyote turned to Carson. "Pay attention, watch where you step, and..."

"Don't reach in dark places," Mike finished.

Little Coyote slung his rife over one massive shoulder, a canteen over the other, and waddled to the huge shop doors. They were mounted on overhead tracks, and he pushed one, squealing, a few feet open. "There's still a few hard-hats inside, and probably some carbide lamps."

The building's interior was dark in contrast to the blazing sun, its old-fashioned windows of little square panes crusted with decades of dust, and it took a moment for his eyes to adjust as Mike, after slinging his shotgun and another canteen, flanked by Carson, who carried the lanterns, followed Little Coyote. The building was mostly empty; concrete floor, furry with dust, wooden workbenches lining the walls, rows of "Chinese-hatted" lights -- dead, of course -- on the spider-webbed rafters, and pieces of old machinery scattered here and there. There was another set of huge doors at the rear of the building, with narrow-gauge tracks leading under them... Mike assumed for mine cart repair back when the shafts were still in use. To both sides of the doors were wooden shelves, bins for parts and supplies, and a row of rusty lockers.

Little Coyote went to a shelf that held a few old miner's helmets. They were made of some kind of composite resembling fiberglass, reddish-blue in color beneath their shrouding of dust, and full-hat style instead of caps. On the front were mounts for lights. Little Coyote examined them, checking the leather headbands. "These look okay," he said, finally selecting three. "Now let's see if there's any lights."

Carson plopped a hat on his head, which completely covered his eyes. Mike laughed. "Here, I'll fix it for you."

Little Coyote checked the lockers, pulling open screechy doors. Most were empty or held useless junk, but finally he opened one with a pile of carbide lamps in the bottom. Mike had seen a few in pawn shops... brass, with three-inch nickel reflectors, striker wheels like cigarette lighters, and hooks to attach to hard-hats. Little Coyote dug through the pile. "These should still work," he said, choosing three.

"What do they burn?" asked Carson, now wearing the helmet Mike had adjusted.

Little Coyote unscrewed the bottom of one, which was like a little cup. "You fill this with carbide. The lamp's upper part is a water tank, and this handle is a valve. You open the valve and water drips onto the carbide. That makes acetylene gas. The gas comes out of this little nozzle in the reflector." He flicked the striker wheel, mak-ing sparks. "You light the gas with this, and adjust the flame with the water valve; the faster it drips, the bigger the flame. They'll burn about three hours until the carbide is all dissolved."

"Steam-punk 'nology," said Carson, taking one of the lamps.

"Where do we get carbide?" asked Mike, who'd put his newsy cap in his pack and adjusted and donned a hard-hat.

Little Coyote pointed to something that looked like a garbage can of rusty, riveted iron. "That's an acetylene generator for a welding torch. It works the same way as these lamps... except you need an oxygen tank to make a flame hot enough to weld. There's probably still some carbide in it."

Mike went to the tank. Its cover was bolted on, but he shed his pack and selected a wrench. While he was unscrewing the bolts, Little Coyote and Carson cleaned the dust-crusted lamps, using old rags from a workbench, and filled them from a canteen. By then Mike had the cover off. "Looks like cement in there."

Little Coyote found a piece of pipe and jabbed the solid stuff, breaking through a crust and revealing what looked like gray gravel. "That's enough to burn these lamps for a month."

He scooped out a handful, and Mike and Carson filled the lamp bases and screwed them back on.

"Like this," said Little Coyote, taking one of the lamps. He opened the valve, waited a minute, then palmed the striker wheel. There was a "pop," and a small white flame jetted from the nozzle.

"That's pretty bright," said Mike.

"I try," said Little Coyote. He adjusted the valve, and the flame slowly lengthened to almost an inch. "Better than most flashlights, but they're mostly used in mines and caves where the air is still. Not much good outside if there's wind."

"You know a lot," said Mike.

"I used to mess with this stuff when I worked here. And the fore-man was an old-timer from back when the shafts were still producing. He taught me lots of things."

Carson had clamped a lamp to his hat. He spread his arms. "Light my fire."

"Wait till we're underground," Little Coyote said. "There's an old tobacco can. Fill it up with carbide in case we're in there awhile."

Carson filled the can, and Mike put it into his pack. Little Coyote mounted his lamp, then adjusted and donned his hat. "Guess we're ready, braves."

FOURTEEN

"How far does this go?" asked Mike, as they stood at the yawning black mouth of the mine after leaving the shop through its rear doorway and following the narrow-gauge track to the vertical foot of a mountain.

"Probably miles," said Little Coyote. "And there'll be lots of branch tunnels."

"Sounds like a lot of walking," said Mike. "Me and Carson could go look for carts."

Little Coyote smiled. "Think I'm out of shape?"

"No, but..."

"Speak any rattlesnake? Or bat?"

"...Oh," said Mike. "Bats, too."

"If I get tired you can carry me."

The boys lit their lamps and lanterns, and Little Coyote led the way, setting the pace with his rippling waddle. The shaft was straight and level, ten feet wide and twelve feet high, the track running down the middle. Heavy electric cables, and pipes that had once supplied compressed air to power drills and jack-hammers, ran along the walls. There were light bulbs overhead, spaced about thirty feet apart.

"Guess we can't turn 'em on?" said Mike.

"The generators are gone," Little Coyote replied. "Along with the air compressors and all the newer machinery."

After a few hundred yards, with daylight fading behind, the air began to cool. "It's getting almost comfortable, at least for me," said Mike, his voice echoing down the tunnel.

Little Coyote nodded. "Stays about seventy all year 'round. And the

86

air is dry, so metal doesn't rust very much. If there are any carts in here, they should be in pretty good shape."

A rattle came out of the darkness, sounding at first like a little motor with loose bearings starting up, then increasing in volume.

"She's over there," said Little Coyote, pointing to the right while waving Mike and Carson left. Mike couldn't see the snake, which might have been concealed in a crack, but Little Coyote stopped to face the eerie sound, softly murmured something, and after a moment it faded away.

"What did you say?" asked Carson.

"We come in peace. She'll pass the word."

"Does that apply to bats?" asked Mike.

"Snakes and bats don't network. But if we meet some bats I'll tell them."

The boys continued on. The sunlit mouth of the shaft dwindled to a tiny speck of light like the end of a classic cartoon. Mike figured they'd walked about half a mile, and there were other tunnels now, branching off on either side, some sloping down, others up, and switches on the track. They continued for maybe another half mile, then Carson stopped at a branch tunnel and peered into its midnight mouth. "Any coyotes in here?"

"Did you see one?" asked Little Coyote.

"Thought I did for a second."

"Some make dens in old mine shafts, but they usually don't go in this far."

"Hey! I think I see a cart!"

Little Coyote and Mike joined Carson, but a heavy plank barred the tunnel, and a dusty sign warned, DANGER KEEP OUT in faded red and yellow.

Carson scrambled under the plank, took off his helmet and held it out, aiming its light down the shaft. "Yeah! There's one!"

Mike and Little Coyote also aimed their lights. There was a cart on rusty rails about fifty feet down the shaft... a heavy, riveted iron box, maybe four feet square and mounted on twelve-inch iron wheels. Carson started for it, but Mike grabbed his shoulder. "What's that sign mean... besides the obvious?"

"The shaft isn't safe," said Little Coyote. "Might collapse, or already has." He scanned the walls and roof with his light. "This part looks pretty solid, but it could be unsafe or collapsed further down, and they left the cart to block the track. ...It's a real old one. Could have been there a hundred years."

"Let's go get it," said Carson.

"Remember, pay attention," Little Coyote said.

"Make educated mistakes," added Mike.

Carson put his helmet back on and started down the track. Mike and Little Coyote ducked under the plank and followed. Reaching the cart, Mike examined it by the light of his lantern: below the box was an iron frame to which the axles and wheels were attached. There was a lever to dump the box -- which was empty except for dust -- and another lever for a brake, now set to hold the cart on the downward-sloping rails.

"There's enough room for all of us to get to Codyville, if we can mount a motor," said Mike.

"Can we do it?" said Carson, "Yeah we can! Let's push it back to the shop."

"Don't touch that!" Little Coyote warned as Carson reached for the brake. "This thing weighs about a quarter-ton and we don't want it getting away." He glanced down the slope where the rails disappeared into total darkness. "No telling how far this tunnel goes, or what shape it's in further down."

"Yeah, Carson," said Mike. "Think before you do something." He knelt to check the wheels. "There's still grease in the journals so it should roll easy on level track... but it's fifty feet uphill to get there."

"We should tie it with the rope," Little Coyote said. "Maybe to the main tunnel track. Then let off the brake and try to push it. If we can't, we'll rig a block and tackle and haul it up that way."

Mike shed his pack and took out the rope.

Carson grabbed one end. "I'll tie it up there."

"Make a good knot," said Little Coyote, as Carson started up the track.

"I know how to tie a knot, duh."

Little Coyote took the rope's other end and tied it to the cart's frame. "Pull it tight," he called to Carson.

"I'm tyin' it to the plank."

"Is it strong enough?" asked Mike.

"It's a four-by-twelve." Carson returned a minute later. "I'll be the brakeman."

"Wait till we get behind it," said Mike, as Carson grabbed the brake lever.

Setting down their lanterns, he and Little Coyote went to the rear of the cart and put their shoulders to the box.

"Keep your feet clear of the rails," Little Coyote warned. "If we can't hold it, the rope's gonna stretch and it'll roll backwards."

"Now?" asked Carson.

"Ready, Mike?" asked Little Coyote.

Mike braced his feet. "Yeah."

Carson released the latch and pushed. "Damn, it's stuck!"

"We've got tools," said Mike..

"No, wait. It moved a little." Carson climbed into the box.

"What are you doing?" asked Little Coyote.

"I can reach it better from here. ...Ready?"

Little Coyote glanced at Mike, who nodded while bracing his feet again. "Okay."

Leaning over, chest-deep in the box, Carson yanked on the lever. There was a gritty metallic squeal and the cart began to roll.

"We can't hold it!" puffed Mike, his feet, like Little Coyote's, slipping on the tunnel floor. "Put on the brake again!"

"Shit, I can't!" yelped Carson, shoving on the lever.

"Mike! Get out of the way!" Little Coyote yelled.

They scrambled clear of the track as the cart rolled on down the slope with Carson trying to lock the brake. The rope began to stretch.

There was a CRACK!

The plank snapped in the middle.

The cart was rolling faster, wheels squealing over the rails, trail-ing the rope down the track.

"Carson! Jump out!" yelled Mike.

"I almost got it!" Carson yelled, still shoving on the lever.

The grade wasn't steep, but the cart was heavy, and rapidly gaining speed.

"JUMP!" yelled Little Coyote.

"I ALMOST GOT IT, DAMMIT!"

Mike dashed after the runaway cart... and heard Ruff's yipping laughter. *A very OLD four-by-twelve.*

"That's not funny!" yelled Mike.

Little Coyote snatched a lantern and lumbered after Mike. Mike had almost caught up with the cart, but tripped on a tie and fell. "JUMP, CARSON!"

"I almost...!"

There was a curve in the tunnel, and Carson's light vanished around it as Mike scrambled back to his feet. "Oh, shit!" he panted as Little Coyote caught up with him. "How far you think this goes down?"

The shriek of iron wheels on rails echoed from the blackness below.

...Then came a reverberating **CLANK!**

"Apparently not very far," Little Coyote puffed.

Mike cupped his hands to his mouth. "CARSON! ARE YOU OKAY?"

For a moment only silence ruled -- the absolute silence of deep underground -- as Mike and Little Coyote stilled their panting breaths and listened. Then Carson's voice echoed up the shaft.

"Yeah, but my light went out."

"Stay where you are! We're coming!" Little Coyote called.

"In your pants?" called Carson.

"Guess he is okay," said Mike, trotting beside Little Coyote as the huge boy wobbled and bobbled along. "...Why did Ruff let that happen?"

"He's your guide, not a guardian angel," Little Coyote puffed. "He won't always give you advice, and he'll let you make mistakes. Sometimes he'll give you a warning, but it might not be obvious unless you think about it."

"What about your coyote?"

"He lets me make mistakes, too. I should have checked that plank."

"But, Carson wouldn't have looked down this tunnel if he hadn't thought he'd seen a coyote."

"The ways of coyotes are subtle."

Mike scanned the walls and roof as they started around the curve. "Does this part look safe?"

"There's a few cracks, but nothing major."

"Wonder what Carson ran into? It sounded like metal, and pretty solid."

"Might be an old steam drill down there. This tunnel's been closed a long time."

Mike felt a stirring in the air, and their lights flickered a little. "What's that?" he asked. "...Not a ghost, I hope?"

"Ventilator shaft." Little Coyote pointed up. "Steam drills had coal-fired boilers, so there had to be ventilation or the mine would fill up with smoke."

"Think there *are* any ghosts in here?"

"I've never heard any stories. This mine had a good safety record. There was only one cave-in that killed anybody... happened in 1897 a few months after the gold robbery. Four miners died and were buried so deep their bodies were never recovered."

Mike shivered. "They're still in here somewhere?"

"The company tried to dig 'em out... had crews working twenty-four-seven. But the tunnel kept caving-in, so after a week they gave up. None of the men who were killed had given any next-of-kin when they'd applied for the job, so there was no one to notify."

"That's kinda sad," said Mike.

Little Coyote shrugged. "At least they have a grave to rest in." His voice hardened a little. "They dug up our burial ground when the mine went open-pit. Blasted our bones with dynamite and crushed 'em up with the ore."

"Sorry," said Mike.

"Don't be, you didn't do it."

"Still sorry," said Mike. Then he pointed as they rounded the curve. "There's a light."

Then Carson's voice called, "Woah! Check this out!"

FIFTEEN

"**W**oah!" echoed Mike, stopping in awe.

There, not fifty feet away, a steam locomotive stood on the rails!

The cart had run into its front coupling, and Carson stood in the cart, his lamp relit, gazing up at the massive machine. It was black like most of its kind, though heavily shrouded in rusty-red dust... and the tarnished brass plate on the front of its boiler bore the number 22.

"It's the Codyville engine!" cried Carson.

"...But... what's it doing here?" said Mike.

"Obviously nothing," said Little Coyote. "And for many moons."

"Seriously," said Mike.

Little Coyote considered. "Just a guess, but after Codyville died, this mine might have used it to pull an ore train into Coyote Flats. But then the Santa Fe pulled up its spur, the mine started smelting ingots, and those were shipped out on trucks, so they didn't need it anymore."

"This is way cool!" exclaimed Carson, who'd climbed to a narrow running-board, scuttled along the boiler, and now leaned out of a cab window. "I'm the engineer!" He pulled the whistle chain. "Woooooo!"

"Who's it belong to now?" asked Mike.

Little Coyote shrugged. "The mining company's out of business. Guess somebody owns the land... which was stolen from us."

Mike went to examine the engine, which almost filled the tunnel. There was only about six inches from the top of its stubby smoke-stack to the tunnel roof, and less than two feet to the walls on each side. Mike went into the narrow space, checking a massive cylinder and the rods and driver wheels. "This is gotta be worth a lot of money! To a steam railroad or a museum. ...And it's still in pretty good shape."

"Because the air is dry." Little Coyote squeezed his bulk between the engine and solid rock.

"Maybe turn sideways?" Mike suggested.

"Don't have a sideways."

"Maybe nobody knew it was down here?" said Carson.

Mike turned to Little Coyote. "Wouldn't the foreman have known? You said he was an old-timer."

"Not *this* old. I'm sure he would have told me if he'd known about it."

Mike continued along the engine and climbed the short ladder into the cab. Little Coyote followed, and Mike and Carson took his hands to help him up the ladder. Mike looked around in the glow of their lights.

"Everything's still here... that's the throttle, the Johnson bar... all the valves and gauges, just like in my book. ...And the tender's still half full of coal." He wiped dust from a sight glass. "There's still some water in the boiler. ...Why would they leave it down here?"

Little Coyote pulled up his jeans, which he'd almost lost in the climb. "It was just old junk back then, and they probably wanted it out of the way. Like you said, steam engines were evolving fast, and this was like a Mac Power PC by 1917." He settled his bulk on the engineer's seat. "And it's narrow gauge, so it couldn't get out of this valley on the Santa Fe track."

Carson had climbed on the coal in the tender, then on top of the water tank, crouching in the space below the tunnel roof. "Why narrow gauge?" he asked. "'Stead of the regular kind?"

"You can make tighter curves," said Mike. "Like the one in this tunnel. Or switch-backing up those mountains."

"Ain't no more train," said Carson, peering into the darkness behind. "An' the tunnel's all caved in back there."

"Probably why they left it here," Little Coyote said. "This tunnel wasn't in use anymore."

"Wonder where the cars went?" said Mike. "In the picture there's a boxcar, two flatcars and a caboose. The train was on a freight run, hauling the gold to Coyote Flats, but the railroad must have had passenger cars so people could get to Codyville."

"Maybe they're still up there?" said Carson.

"Look in the water tank," said Mike. "There should be a cover that opens."

"Yeah, I see it," said Carson. There was a metallic creak, and Carson's voice echoed as he looked in. "It's empty."

"Figured it would be," said Mike. "After all this time. There's only water in the boiler 'cause it couldn't evaporate." He looked around the cab again at the valves and gauges. "You need lots of water to run a steam engine. The boiler has to be kept full. There's a pump... also called an injector... to pull water out of the tender."

Little Coyote smiled. "Are you thinking what I think you're thinking?"

"If they called 'em sad meals children wouldn't buy them?"

"Seriously."

"...Well..." said Mike, still gazing around at all the controls and recognizing many of them from illustrations in his book. "Like I said, we'd need lots of water, even just to fire up the boiler." He checked the sight glass again. "It's about a quarter full. That would make enough steam to run the injector, but there's no water in the tender. And if the crown plate goes dry... that's the top of the fire box... the boiler could explode."

Little Coyote looked thoughtful. "Assuming we had water, what would we do next?"

"Pump the boiler full, then we'd be ready to roll. Theoretically, anyhow."

"What's that mean?" asked Carson, jumping down on the coal, then climbing into the fireman's seat and lighting a cigarette.

"If everything else was okay," said Mike. He brushed the dust off a pressure gauge, its needle showing zero, then tugged the throttle lever. "Assuming there was nothing wrong when they left it here, it still hasn't run for a hundred years. We'd have to get it back in shape... clean the dust out of everything, polish up the piston rods, fill the oil cups on the drivers, grease the slider shoes, put new packing in all these valves, make new leather seals for the injector, check out the air brake compressor. ...And a million other things."

Carson pulled an overhead rope, and a clang echoed up the tunnel. "The bell still works."

"That's about the only thing we wouldn't have work on," said Mike. "...Assuming we had water. This engine uses about five gallons to make enough steam to go a mile. That's a small tender 'cause the Codyville line was only fifty miles long, but the tank holds a thousand gallons."

"You know a lot, too," said Carson.

"That's 'cause I read, try it sometime."

"So, how could we fill up the tank?" asked Carson. "It would take a hundred years if we used our canteens."

Little Coyote was still looking thoughtful. "The mine's lower tunnels are probably flooded. That's why they needed pumps."

"Those one-cylinder engines?" asked Mike.

"And there's a lot of old hose."

Mike fingered the throttle lever. "We really might be able to do it."

"Get this thing runnin'?" asked Carson. "An' go to Codyville?"

"I don't know about that," said Mike. "Trying to run it up those mountains on a track that hasn't been used since 1917. ...But, maybe to Little Coyote's house."

"Our very own railroad!" said Carson. "Hey, we'd be real steam punks!"

"We'd have to check out the track," said Mike. "See if all the ties are solid, the rails are still spiked down and aligned. ...But... if we can get it fired up, we should run it into the shop first and clean and fix everything."

"Won't there be a lotta smoke if we start a fire down here?"

"Check your cigarette," said Mike. "The smoke's drifting up the tunnel. There's a ventilator shaft."

"So," said Little Coyote. "Besides water, what's the first thing we need?"

"My book," said Mike. "Um, think our guides would approve?"

"Like you said, we wouldn't be here if Carson hadn't seen a coyote."

SIXTEEN

"Here's a roll of packing," Little Coyote called.

It was about two hours later, and Mike and Little Coyote were back in the copper mine's shop. They'd found a drum of turbine oil, a ten-gallon tub of machinery grease, a brass oil can with a twelve-inch spout, and a roll of crocus cloth. They'd unloaded Carson's bike from the Euclid, and Carson had gone to get Mike's book.

"Found some more rags," Mike called from a corner. "We're gonna need a lot of those. And here's one of those old-time pumps." He knelt beside the machine, which resembled an antique coffee-grinder, and spun its heavy flywheel. "It's still free, and there's compression... OW!"

"What happened?" Little Coyote called.

"The magneto still sparks."

Little Coyote came over pushing an ancient hand-truck with a wooden frame and iron wheels. "Let's bring it out where we can see better."

Mike glanced to a dust-crusted window, where evening sunlight filtered in. "It's gonna be getting dark soon."

"I'll drive my truck in and turn on the lights."

They wrestled the pump onto the hand-truck and pushed it across the floor. "There's plenty of hose in the junkyard," Little Coyote said. "All we have to do is find another lower tunnel, take the pump down where it's flooded and run the hose up to the tender."

Mike indicated the hand-truck. "We can rig this to roll on the rails so it'll be easy to push... make a wider axle from a piece of pipe, and I found a couple of mine cart wheels. But this engine burns gas and your truck is diesel."

96

"We can use some gas from Carson's bike to see if we can get it started."

"There's a five gallon can of spare gas on my dad's Rover," said Mike. "Carson could go back for that."

"That'll run this pump about four hours." Little Coyote brushed dust from a small brass plate. "Pumps 250 gallons an hour."

"Just what we need to fill the tender. ...Another coincidence?"

"I'm starting to lean toward signs."

They stopped in the fan of yellow sunlight slanting through the open front doors, and Mike pushed up his cap to wipe sweat from his eyes. "We only have to do basic stuff to fire the locomotive and run it out of the mine... clean the dust out of moving parts, get the injector working, fill the driver and cylinder oil cups, grease the sliders, and polish the rods so they don't tear the seals. We'll do the major work in here."

There was bratty snarl, and Carson rocketed through the doorway, spewing dust across the floor and skidding to a stop. "Here's the book."

"Did you tell my dad what we found?" asked Mike.

"He wasn't home." Carson flashed a buck-toothed grin. "Mom 'vited him to dinner."

"...Oh," said Mike.

SEVENTEEN

"Almost full!" called Carson, crouching on the tender and peering into the water tank. "It's gonna run over soon."

"How long has it been?" asked Mike.

Carson checked his watch. "'Bout three hours since we started the pump."

"That's funny," said Mike. "Must hold less than a thousand gallons... but that's what the specifications say."

There was a gurgling sound. "It's runnin' over," said Carson.

"That's okay," said little Coyote, his rolly mass squeezed in the narrow space between the tunnel wall and the engine as he filled the last of the driver cups with the long-spouted oil can. "The pump will run out of gas in a while."

"So, we're ready to light the fire?"

"Almost," said Mike, who was in the cab tightening the packing nuts on the many boiler valves. "Some of these will probably leak, but we'll re-pack 'em in the shop."

"What's next?" asked Carson, jumping down on the coal.

Mike indicated a short-handled shovel. "Clean the clinkers out of the firebox."

Carson knelt at the iron door. "Mean, I gotta get in there?"

"You're just the right size."

"Nah, I'm too fat."

"You wish," laughed Little Coyote.

"I'll do it," said Mike.

"Nah," said Carson. "Keep workin' on the important stuff."

"That's important, too," said Mike. "We need a hot fire to build up steam as fast as we can. Even with the vent shaft there's gonna be a lot of smoke, and we have to get out of this tunnel before it gets too thick. It shouldn't be so bad once we're up on level track."

"What about the mine cart?" asked Carson.

"We'll push it out as we go."

Carson unbuckled his gun and hung it on the throttle bar, then squirmed into the firebox, squeezing his belly over the rim. "Ain't you gonna say this is good exercise? 'Gettin' active,' an' all that shit?"

"Nah," said Mike. "It's good 'cause we're doing something cool."

"The headlight's acetylene," called Little Coyote. "Works the same way as our lamps... fill the generator with carbide. Should be a water valve in the cab to control the flame."

Mike paged through his book. "Yeah, this little one."

Carson's voice came from the firebox. "Thought they didn't work outside?"

"The flame's behind a glass lens," said Mike.

"...Oh, yeah." There was a scrape of the shovel, and clinkers scattered across the cab floor. "What's for lunch?"

"Guess it is about time," said Mike. "Hard to keep track when you're underground."

"And time warps fast when you're having fun," Little Coyote added.

"Is that an Apache saying?"

"Rough translation. I'll make us some paleface food... ham and cheese sandwiches on white bread with mayonnaise."

"Hey," said Carson poking his head from the sooty firebox. "I'm the only paleface here."

"Not anymore," said Mike.

The tunnel was fairly well lit: in addition to the lights on their hats and the trio of lanterns, they'd brought a few other carbide lamps and set them around the locomotive. There was also a kerosene lamp in the cab. They'd worked in the shop the night before until around ten o'clock, gotten the pump engine running, and rigged the hand-truck to roll on the rails. Then they'd gone to the bunkhouse -- a long low building of rusty tin with rows of double-decked wooden bunks -- where Little Coyote had cooked cheese-burgers on a pot-bellied stove. They'd washed their supper down with Coke and had Gansitos for desert, saving the beer to celebrate when the locomotive was out of the mine.

They'd gone to sleep around midnight, after Mike had told one his father's ghost stories by the glow of a lantern. Mike had been tired, of course, but it was a better tired somehow -- maybe a more satisfying tired -- than he'd ever felt after working-out. Still, he'd awakened a few hours later, moonlight beaming through dusty windows, hearing the laughter of coyotes outside. Little Coyote and Carson were asleep in the bunks beside him, lying like Mike in just their jeans atop the Indian blankets, but Mike got up and went to the door. He'd quietly lifted the latch and pulled the door gently open so its hinges didn't squeak, recalling what Little Coyote had said... the brothers hanging out at the mine. There were maybe twenty of them prowling around in the silvery light. He'd recognized Ruff amongst them because he seemed to glow... which, being a spirit, seemed logical. Ruff had looked enigmatically sly. *You're on the right track*, he'd said, then vanished.

Mike had returned to bed and slept until around seven. Little Coyote was already up, frying sausages, eggs and potatoes, while coffee boiled in a battered pot. After breakfast they'd gone in the mine, found a flooded tunnel, set up the pump and rigged the hose. Then they'd worked on the locomotive. Using leather from hard-hat bands, Mike made new seals for the injector. Then he'd oiled the throttle linkage, the Johnson bar and the air brake compressor. Then he'd checked all the boiler valves, pausing to consult his book to find the function of each. Little Coyote had polished the rods, wiped and greased the slider shoes, and filled the drivers and piston oil cups, while Carson, armed with rags and a brush, cleaned the dust out of mechanisms.

They had brought in one of the ice chests, and Little Coyote now washed his hands at the overflowing tender, then made sandwiches. Carson shoveled the last of the clinkers and, now almost as black as Mike, wiggled out of the firebox. They ate their lunch in the cab and shared a box of Gansitos, Little Coyote in the engineer's seat, Carson in the fireman's, and Mike perched on a window sill. Carson gulped the last of his Coke and lit a cigarette. "When'll we be ready to roll?"

Mike finished his Coke and paged through the book. "We can lay the fire now. Maybe an hour to build up steam... full head is 120 pounds."

"Who gets to be the engineer?"

"Mike," said Little Coyote. "He's the one who knows about trains."

"All I know came out of this book." Mike offered it to Little Coyote. "Here's the chapter on starting... Johnson bar forward and full cut-off. Brake handle off. And open the throttle easy or you'll get a traction-break. This was a primitive engine, even in 1897. They were mostly built for switchers, not to go very fast."

"How fast will it go?" asked Carson.

"Maybe forty-five tops with those little drivers, but we'll have to go slow in here. After starting it's pretty simple... pull out the throttle to go faster, push it in to slow down, and pull the brake handle to stop. You also have to adjust the cut-off, but that's not important to get out of here."

Carson added, "An' pull the chain to blow the whistle."

Little Coyote took the book. "You saying I should drive it?"

"It really belongs to you," said Mike. "And if we can get it to your house, you could sell it and go on a cruise."

"Yeah," agreed Carson. "Us palefaces stole your land, an' this is givin' somethin' back."

Little Coyote smiled. "Don't see any pale faces here. And this belongs to all of us. We'll take turns being engineer on the way to my house."

Mike picked up the shovel. "I'll be the fireman this time."

"What am I this time?" asked Carson.

"The brakeman," said Mike.

"I wasn't a very good brakeman last time."

"Yeah, you were," said Little Coyote. "You kept trying to stop your train when you could have jumped off."

"And that's how we found this engine," said Mike.

"So, what can I do now?"

"Clean the headlight," said Mike. "We're gonna need it to see through the smoke."

Little Coyote opened the book. "I'll start reading my engineer course."

Mike knelt to inspect the firebox: Carson had done a good job and the grate and ash pit were clean. Taking a broom they'd found in the shop, he swept the clinkers out of the cab, while Carson climbed out on the running-board and went to polish the headlight. Then Mike built a starter fire with wood from dynamite boxes and magazines they'd found in the bunkhouse, including several *Playboys*, and lit it with his lamp. After watching a centerfold burst into flame, he shoveled coal evenly onto the grate. There were creaks of expanding iron as the boiler began to warm up. Smoke curled lazily out the stack and drifted up the tunnel, drawn by the ventilator shaft. Mike shoveled more coal to build up the fire, then checked the water in the sight glass.

"Hope the injector works, or we'll have to put the fire out before the crown plate goes dry. There's a lever to dump the fire in an emergency, but that's usually done while moving. Could be dangerous in here."

Little Coyote tapped the pressure gauge with a fingertip, its needle still on zero. "The book says we need at least thirty pounds to run the injector."

"Should be enough water in the boiler for that."

Little Coyote watched the gauge, its needle still showing nothing, though heat from the fire was filling the cab, while smoke was swirling out of the stack and starting to haze the air. Carson coughed, climbing down from the headlight and coming back on a running-board. "Gettin' pretty smoky up there."

Little Coyote tapped the gauge again: its needle quivered a moment, then slowly began to move, hovering first at five PSI, then creeping up toward ten. Mike re-checked the sight glass, noting the water level was dropping. A wisp of steam curled out of a valve, and he tightened its packing nut, then handed the wrench to Carson.

"The generator tank is under the right side running-board. "Clean it out and fill it with carbide." He waved smoke away from his face. "We're gonna need that light soon."

"Aye aye, sir," said Carson.

Little Coyote laughed. "That's another story."

The bitter black smoke was growing denser, dimming the lamp

and lantern flames. Mike's eyes were beginning to water. "It wouldn't have been very bad backing down the slope in here. Or they could have banked the fire and let it roll down from the main tunnel."

Little Coyote nodded, still scanning the book, held close to his light. "And they probably didn't think they'd ever use it again and have to drive it out of here."

The pressure gauge needle had risen to twenty and was slowly creeping upward, though the water level was steadily falling. Mike pitched more coal in the firebox. The temperature in the cab was still rising, the boiler radiating heat, and Mike was starting to sweat. Carson called, "I filled the generator, how do I light the light?"

Mike opened a small valve. "Should be enough pressure to start the water."

Little Coyote added, "Wait a few minutes to generate gas, then open the lens and light it like the lamp on your hat."

The pressure gauge had reached thirty pounds, the sight glass level still dropping. "Here goes," said Mike, and opened a valve.

There was a hiss beneath the cab, then a few hesitant clicks. Mike opened the valve another turn and the clicking increased to a faster rhythm. Mike watched the glass as the smoke grew thicker. "Yeah, it's rising, we're getting water. I'll start the compressor." He opened another valve, and a dog-like panting began.

"Got it lit!" called Carson, and coughed. "But the smoke's gettin' really bad up here!"

Mike and Little Coyote peered forward. The smoke looked scary now in the bluish beam of the headlight, like a roiling, seething, ebony cloud filling the tunnel ahead. Mike realized, if something went wrong and the locomotive wouldn't move, they'd have to get through that on foot to ever see daylight again.

He wiped his eyes, now streaming tears that streaked the dust on his cheeks. "I hope Ruff was right."

"About what?" asked Little Coyote.

Mike coughed. "I saw him last night outside the bunkhouse. He said I was on the right track. ...Or maybe he meant we all were."

"But of course he didn't say to where." Little Coyote put down the book and watched the pressure gauge. "We can start with ninety pounds 'cause we're not pulling a train... and we've just about got it."

Mike leaned from the fireman's window. He could barely see the headlight glow through the ever-thickening smoke. "Carson!" he called, "c'mon! Get in!"

"What about the ice chest?"

"Put it in the cart and c'mon!"

A few seconds later, Carson scrambled into the cab, wiping his eyes and coughing. Mike touched Little Coyote's shoulder. "Go for it. ...Carson, get in the fireman's seat so you're not in my way."

Little Coyote set the cut-off lever and gripped the throttle bar. He eased it out a little, and there was a hiss from the cylinders. The locomotive trembled, and there were rusty creaking sounds of ancient iron coming to life.

"Give it some more," panted Mike, feeding the firebox.

Little Coyote pulled the throttle. Suddenly there were metallic screams and blasts of steam as the drivers spun, shaking and rocking the engine.

Mike coughed, the bitter smoke burning his throat. "Traction-break. Shut it down and start again."

Again Little Coyote eased out the throttle. Now there was a chuff of steam and the locomotive began to inch forward. "More advice would be helpful."

"Just feel it," said Mike. "You have to run a steam engine by feel. They're double-acting cylinders, so the drivers won't dead-center."

"I guess that's a good thing." Little Coyote pulled more throttle. There was another hissing chuff and the locomotive crept ahead. ...Then two chuffs a little faster. Then three... four... five... six... Then a more rhythmic four-beat pulse as their speed increased to a walking pace.

"Keep her going," panted Mike, sweatily feeding the fire.

The smoke was black around them now, their lights only dim yellow sparks, the firebox a ruddy square. "I can't see anything," called Little Coyote, leaning out the window.

"We know the track is clear," coughed Mike. "And we set the switch in the main tunnel. Keep going until we're outside."

Their speed increased a little more, the chugging a steady

quadruple throb as pistons thrust and pulled the rods. The blast pipe echo was deafening as smoke mushroomed from the tunnel roof and gushed into the cab. The wheels squealed along the rails as they chuffed and puffed around the curve. They were still running blind in smothering smoke when the wheels clanked over something.

"That was the switch," panted Mike. "We're in the main tunnel now."

"Can I ring the bell?" asked Carson.

"Go for it," said Little Coyote.

Carson pulled the rope, and clanging echoed down the tunnel. The smoke was thinning a little as their speed increased on level track to maybe five miles-an-hour. Little Coyote eased in the throttle.

"See?" panted Mike. "It's mostly feel. ...Like riding a horse, I guess."

Little Coyote laughed. "I'd never inflict myself on a horse... assuming I could *get* on a horse. I sway-backed your great-uncle's mule when I was only ten."

"Who needs horses," laughed Carson. "We're in the steam age now!"

EIGHTEEN

For the first time in a hundred years, billowing smoke and spewing steam, engine Number 22 of the Coyote Valley and Codyville Railroad came chugging into sunlight, bursting out of a midnight cloud gushing from the mine shaft.

"Blow the whistle," said Carson.

Little Coyote pulled the chain, and a WOOOOOOOOOOOOOO echoed over the silent desert, a mighty yet also haunting cry that only tortoises remembered.

"Steam rules!" yelled Carson, thrusting a fist at the sky.

"Should I stop?" asked Little Coyote as, still at about five miles an hour, and pushing the mine cart rattling ahead, they chuffed down the rails toward the mine shop, clanking and rocking past the switch that led to the Codyville line.

Mike, dripping sweat and streaked with coal dust, leaned on the shovel and panted, "Let's take her inside."

"An' have some beer," added Carson. He patted his belly and laughed. "Feels like I lost twenty pounds today."

Mike smiled. "We'll have to get you back in shape so there's more of you to love."

"Aw."

They had already opened the doors and, wheels squealing, blast pipe spouting, and still shedding ruddy dust from its flanks, the locomotive entered the shop for service a century overdue. Little Coyote shut down the throttle and eased the brake lever back. Brake shoes clamped to the drivers with gritty teeth-grinding shrieks, and the locomotive creaked to a halt. The cart rolled on about twenty feet to clank a buffer at the end of the track.

"What now?" asked Little Coyote. "I assume we just don't turn off a switch."

Mike consulted the book. "The fire will go out by itself. Open that valve: it'll blow out the boiler tubes and get rid of sediment."

Little Coyote opened the valve, and twin clouds of steam blasted out in front of the dripping cylinders, whipping twisters of swirling dust across the concrete floor.

Mike watched the pressure gauge drop as the hissing began to subside, then checked the sight glass. "We'll pump more water into the boiler so it cools down slow. Probably be a few hours til everything is cool enough to start checking out and do more cleaning."

"I'll get the beer!" said Carson, climbing down from the cab.

Mike turned toward the afternoon sunlight slanting through the front doorway. "This would be a good time to check out the track to Little Coyote's."

"Yeah," agreed Carson, returning with a sixer of frosty San Miguels. "Be a bitch if we can't get this out of here! What good's a train if there's nowhere to go?"

Little Coyote accepted a beer, popped the cap and drank. "I used to walk the track to the mine. There's a tunnel on the spur through a mountain shoulder, and a few trestles over washes, but they looked in pretty good shape."

"The rail alignment's important," said Mike, also taking a bottle. "Even if the ties are good, the rails could have shifted in all this time, and two inches off could derail us."

Little Coyote sipped more beer. "What about using the mine cart? The track's almost level to my house, so it should roll pretty easy, and if it derails so would this engine."

"I can tow it with my bike," said Carson, gulping from his bottle. "You guys can ride in the box."

"Good idea," said Mike, and studied the shop's heavy rafters. "We can rig a block and tackle to lift the cart off the tracks, then push it around behind the engine and back onto the rails. If the track is okay to Little Coyote's, you can get more gas for your bike at the store and we should be back here in a few hours."

Still on schedule, said Ruff.

"...Did you hear that?" asked Mike.

"What?" asked Carson.

Little Coyote smiled. "Guess it's between you and him now."

"What about your guide?" asked Mike.

"Could be a coyote conspiracy."

"Mean, they're testin' him?" asked Carson.

"Maybe they're testing all of us."

NINETEEN

"Are we ready to roll?" asked Carson.

Like the other boys he was covered with dust and streak-ed with oil, his face and hair blackened by soot so he looked like his own minstrel show. It was evening on the day after they'd driven the engine into the shop, and the air was cooling a little as darkness settled outside. They'd been working on the locomotive since having breakfast at dawn -- sausage, eggs, and fried potatoes -- pausing for lunch around noon -- beef and cheese chimichangas provided by Little Coyote's sister -- then for supper at six o'clock of chorizo burritos and chicken tamales, also supplied by Dancing Fox.

They'd inspected the track yesterday, Little Coyote and Mike in the cart watching the rails for alignment, while Carson towed them with his bike hitched by ten feet of rope. He'd worn Mike's jeans to protect his legs from sagebrush and cactus on the line, while Mike wore only his cap, sneaks, and a loincloth... the latter made by Little Coyote, cut from one of their blankets.

The spur to the Codyville track ran south along the feet of the mountains, and a tunnel bored through a shoulder of rock just before the mainline junction. A rattlesnake had let them pass after Little Coyote's greeting.

North of the junction the rails ascended to begin switch-backing up the mountains, but the boys took the track that angled south-west, heading for the water tank at Little Coyote's house. There was a slight downgrade so the cart trundled easily after Carson. They'd found two sledgehammers in the shop, and Mike, acting as brake-man to keep the cart from rolling too fast, had stopped several times along the way;

he and Little Coyote dismounting to pound loose spikes back into place. Mike was no expert on rail beds, his only experience H.O. scale, but the track seemed in almost strangely good shape for being abandoned a hundred years. The rail alignment was almost perfect, and the trestles over washes and gullies, though heavily weathered, still stood strong.

As they'd approached the first of these, Little Coyote had pointed ahead. "That's where the robbery happened, just across this trestle."

Mike had studied the land, which looked like Mordor in *Lord Of The Rings*, bristling with flinty ridges, littered with jagged rocks and boulders tumbled down from the mountains, and cut by sheer-sided gulches as if raked by gargantuan claws. How could a wagon have gotten away loaded with a ton of gold?

They'd inspected the trestle and then rolled on, the terrain becoming gentler on the valley floor. There were occasional clumps of cactus that Carson couldn't ride through. Then they would stop, get behind the cart, and bull their way through pushing it. All these stops took time of course; and though it was only three miles from the mine, the sun was behind the western mountains and rosy twilight painting the sky when they finally reached Little Coyote's house.

His sister was just rolling up in her battered International, and had asked about their adventure... to which Little Coyote only replied they were bringing home a "heap-big surprise." Mike had looked toward his own house, seeing the Land Rover parked in front and a light the living room window.

Carson had asked, "You gonna tell your dad?"

"Nah," Mike had said. "It'll really be a heap-big surprise when he sees us chugging out of the desert."

Dancing Fox had made a huge supper of beef and green chili enchiladas, chicken tostadas, refried beans, rice, and corn tortillas, with guacamole and sour cream, followed by hefty portions of flan. Then Little Coyote and Mike had dutifully washed the dishes, while Carson had ridden to the store to put more gas in his bike. Then they'd loaded it into the pickup, and Dancing Fox had driven them back to the copper mine, after packing ample provisions into a dynamite box. Mike caught a glimpse of his dad at work as they'd passed his house, and had silently wished him inspiration on his new ghost story.

After Dancing Fox had left, the boys went into the shop in a kind of unspoken agreement to be sure the locomotive was there, as if, being almost too good to be true, it might have somehow vanished. But there it was, big and black -- if somewhat rusty -- its boiler still warm as they touched it to be absolutely sure.

"How does it radiate?" Mike had asked.

"Off the positive scale," Little Coyote replied.

"You gonna sell it?" Carson had asked. "An' go on a cruise like you always wanted?"

Little Coyote had smiled at Mike. "Be cool to have our own railroad."

"Heap-big cool," Mike had agreed. "Even if only three miles long."

"There's twenty more miles of track into Coyote Flats. An' thirty more up to Codyville," Carson had reminded.

Little Coyote had laughed. "One adventure at a time."

Mike had nodded. "Don't start building your layout till you get your locomotive home."

Then they'd gone to the bunkhouse for a well-earned good night's rest.

Now, wiping oil from his hands with a rag, Mike regarded the locomotive, cleaned of dust, oiled and greased; and even its number 22 gleaming in lamp and lantern glow. "She should be ready." Then he faced the darkness beyond the shop's rear doorway. "But, maybe we should wait till morning."

"We know the track is okay," said Carson.

Mike turned to Little Coyote. "What do you think?"

"Full moon tonight... the coyote's sun... so we'd able to see pretty well."

"An' we got the headlight," said Carson.

Mike nodded. "And it'll be cooler shoveling coal. If we fire her up now, we can leave in an hour."

"So, what are we waitin' for," said Carson, climbing into the cab. "Who gets to be the engineer first?"

"You," said Little Coyote. "I'll be the fireman this time."

"Yay!"

"And I'll be the brakeman," said Mike. "Until we get to the main line."

Little Coyote said, "Then Mike will be the engineer."

"An' I'll be the fireman," said Carson.

"As far as the robbery site," said Mike. "Then Little Coyote drives her home."

Ruff laughed from somewhere. *And everyone gets a heap-big surprise.*

TWENTY

"We still have plenty of water," Little Coyote said, closing the tender's cover, then easing his bulk down onto the coal and taking up the shovel.

Mike was tightening a leaky valve. "We didn't use much getting out of the mine. ...Funny, I checked the capacity plate and it does say a thousand gallons, but I'm *sure* we put in less than that if the pump pumped two-fifty gallons an hour."

Carson was in the engineer's seat, reading Mike's book by the golden glow of the kerosene lamp in the cab. "Maybe it pumped faster?"

"Or there's sediment in the tank?" Little Coyote suggested, adding a scoop of coal to the fire.

Mike checked the steam pressure gauge, its needle at seventy pounds and climbing, while smoke drifted up from the stack into the shop's lofty rafters. "There's a big drain valve on the tank, and they would have flushed any sediment out, probably at least once a week, so the boiler tubes wouldn't clog up."

Carson said, "But maybe they stopped takin' care of it when they didn't need it no more."

"You might be right," said Mike, wiping sweat from his eyes as the temperature rose in the cab. There were creaks and ticks of expanding iron and a low rumbling sound as water boiled. "Or they might have done some repairs," he said, turning to study the tender. "The sides of the tank go around the coal box, and maybe they sealed 'em off because they were leaking or rusted inside, so it does hold less than a thousand gallons. That wouldn't have mattered on a fifty mile line.

113

There had to be a water tank up in Codyville, plus the one at Little Coyote's house, and probably one in Coyote Flats."

"Yeah," said Carson. "It's at the ol' station. ...Be cool if we got a passenger car. We could charge people for rides on our railroad. Maybe up to Codyville."

"That would be cool," agreed Mike. "But it would take a *lot* of money to start up something like that. We'd have to get everything legal... buy the line into Codyville, get insurance and all that stuff. Probably need a million dollars."

"I don't know about you guys," Little Coyote said. "But I'm happy with three miles of track and a locomotive to run on it."

"Speakin' of which," said Carson. "When are we gonna get goin'?"

They had started the fire an hour ago, and the pressure was now nearing 100 pounds. They had loaded Carson's bike on the tender; and Little Coyote's yellow boy and Mike's shotgun were in the cab, while Carson packed his Colt. They had put out most of the lanterns and lamps, leaving the engine's headlight beam and the glow of the lamp in the cab. Mike had found a red railroad lantern underneath the fireman's seat, and hung it on the back of the tender.

"What's that for?" Carson had asked.

"To warn ghost trains," Mike had replied.

"...You're kiddin'... right?"

Little Coyote had laughed. "Better safe than haunted."

Mike checked the gauge again. The pressure was nearing 120, and a wisp of steam was beginning to rise from the safety valve atop a sand dome. "Guess we're ready." He relit one of their lanterns and climbed down from cab. "Back her out past the switch. I'll signal when to stop."

"Okay," said Carson. "Johnson bar back, an' full cut-off."

"You know a lot," said Mike.

"That's 'cause I read. ...Should I blow the whistle?"

Little Coyote smiled. "Of course."

Again, a mighty yet ghostly cry echoed over the silent desert, and even more haunting in the night.

Carson pushed the brake handle forward. There was a hiss as shoes released. Then, leaning from the window and looking rear-ward for Mike's signals, he eased the throttle out. Again came a hiss, this of steam, then a slow CHUFF and the engine crept backward. Another chuff, a little faster. Then... one...two...three... four... and the locomotive emerged into moonlight.

Mike, now bathed in the ruby glow of the lantern on the tender, waved his light in slow circles until the engine passed the switch, then he swung it back and forth, signaling Carson to stop. Then he shifted the rails to the spur and climbed back into the cab. Little Coyote took the shovel. "Go for it, Carson."

Carson reset the Johnson bar, released the brake and opened the throttle. Again came the slow chugging one...two...three... four... and, bright beam lighting the track ahead, engine number 22 of the Coyote Valley and Codyville Railroad -- wheels rumbling, blast pipe spouting, gushing black smoke at the silver full moon -- puffed away into the desert.

Carson blew the whistle again, and maybe, besides the tortoises, a few ghosts remembered its cry.

"Should I give her more throttle?" he asked, leaning from the window in the classic engineer pose.

"A little," said Mike, sitting in the fireman's seat while Little Coyote shoveled coal. He glanced at the speed indicator, its needle barely off the pin. "No more than ten on this old track. Better safe than derailed."

Carson eased out a bit more throttle, and the chugging grew faster. "Should I pull down the cut-off?" he asked. "We're on level track an' rollin', so full cut-off is wastin' steam."

"Yeah," said Mike. "And keep on reading."

Carson strained on the bar against the pulse of the pistons, and the engine steadied at ten miles an hour, rocking a bit on the rail bed, wheels click-clacking over the joints, and feeling alive and eager to run after its century sleep.

Mike leaned from his window as they neared the tunnel. "Do you see that?"

"What?" asked Carson.

Mike turned to Little Coyote, who'd leaned from the cab behind him, but only got a smile.

Ruff sat to one side of the tunnel mouth. As usual he looked enigmatically sly, but held an old-fashioned railroad watch, its chain in his teeth, the watch cover open, though Mike couldn't read the time as they passed.

Right on schedule, said Ruff.

TWENTY ONE

"That was over too soon," sighed Carson, bringing the engine to a stop by pushing in the throttle and pulling the air brake lever as they clanked past the switch on the Codyville line.

Mike laughed. "Time does warp fast when you're having fun."

Little Coyote gave Carson the shovel and settled onto the fireman's seat, while Mike took Carson's place. Like many people with model trains, he'd dreamed of driving a real one, and now that dream had come true! He pushed up his cap a little, released the brake and eased out the throttle. Again, the slow rhythmic chuffing began, and he adjusted the cut-off, the locomotive gaining speed as the track descended gently toward the valley floor. He'd read that a steam locomotive was like a living thing, and it really felt that way, rocking and rumbling over the rails, especially out in the desert night beneath a billion diamond stars with the full moon beaming down.

"Blow the whistle," said Carson, adding more coal to the fire.

Mike did, and a tingle ran down his spine as the haunting cry echoed out. A hand on the throttle, an arm out the window, the warm night breeze caressing his face as the engine pulsed and puffed along, he wished this time would last forever. But then they were nearing the first trestle, and he called to Little Coyote, "Time for you to take her home."

He was about to ease in the throttle when he saw something ahead. "You see *that?*" he yelled.

"I do," said Little Coyote in his matter-of-fact tone of voice.

"What?" asked Carson. He leaned from the cab behind Mike. "...What the hell!"

117

"You see it, too?" asked Mike.

"There's a *wagon* on the tracks just across the trestle! With four horses! ...An' somebody with a lantern!"

Mike's first thought was to stop, and he almost reached for the brake. But then he turned to Little Coyote. "Tell me that's real, okay? And we won't run through it like smoke."

Little Coyote looked thoughtful. "We can't run though it, that's not what happened."

"...What do you mean?" asked Mike, a hand now gripping the brake lever.

"Shit!" cried Carson, checking his watch. "It's after midnight on June 13th! This is when the robbery happened in 1897!" He dropped the shovel and pulled his gun. "But it ain't gonna happen again! Keep goin', Mike! Give her more throttle an' bust right through it!"

"It *will* happen," said Little Coyote. "Because we have to let it happen. Stop her, Mike."

Carson's mouth dropped open. "But, we're gonna get robbed by *ghosts!*"

"Maybe it's real," said Mike, squinting ahead in the moonlight. "And we don't wanna wreck it or hurt anybody." He put in the throttle and pulled the brake.

"It's real enough," said Little Coyote.

"NO!" howled Carson. "That's a *ghost* wagon, an' that guy's a ghost! ...An' there's three other ghosts hidin' somewhere to rob us when we stop!"

Little Coyote shrugged. "What isn't real about that?"

Mike was scared, yet almost laughed. "Rob us of what? We don't have the gold."

"I gots twenty dollars. That was a lotta money back then."

"...I think I get it," said Mike, turning to Little Coyote. "This is a residual haunting, like in one of my dad's stories. Those ghosts are like actors in an old movie. They've been dead for a lot of years, but their images are trapped in the film and it's replaying tonight."

"A logical explanation... at least for the living," said Little Coyote. "But, welcome to the spirit world where living logic may not apply."

Carson reluctantly holstered his gun. "Mean, them ghosts only think they're seein' a train like on the night they robbed it? An' they're just gonna act it out?"

Mike brought the engine to a stop, brake shoes squealing softly, about fifty feet from the big ore wagon... which looked very solid and real despite the coal smoke on the warm night breeze swirling around and hazing the headlight. So did the team of horses, who seemed to be waiting patiently. ...And so did the figure holding the lantern; though Mike caught only a glimpse of him before the safety valve lifted and spewed a misty cloud of steam. Mike opened a valve to release more steam from the pipes in front of the cylinders, shrouding the figure in ghostly white as it started toward them. "That's what residual hauntings do. But sometimes you can interact... sort of double-act with them."

Carson kept a hand on his gun. "I ain't double-actin' with no goddamn ghosts!"

Little Coyote said, "We might not have a choice about that."

"...Sooo... what do we do?" asked Carson. "Act like we think the train crew did in 1897?"

"They might not even see us," said Mike. "Or react to anything we do. Residual hauntings aren't self-aware."

He closed the valve as the pressure dropped, and desert silence settled except for the pant of the air compressor. Steam still drifted around the engine, hiding the approaching figure, though Mike could see the glow of its lantern. Then he heard the crunch of its footsteps on the rail bed gravel... why would a ghost's steps crunch?

Carson was still gripping his gun, and backed away from the side of the cab. "W-what's it gonna say?"

Little Coyote was still sitting calmly in the fireman's seat, his face only looking thoughtful in the glow of the cab's lamp. "If Mike is right, it will probably say the wagon is stuck and ask for our help."

"What's it gonna look like?"

Mike was also wondering. Though he'd only glimpsed the figure, already half obscured by smoke before being shrouded in steam, it hadn't been what he'd expected somehow. ...Of course, never seeing a ghost before, he hadn't known *what* to expect, but assumed a residual haunting -- like the wagon and horses -- would look like it had in the past. And, because these ghosts were outlaws from 1897, he'd expected western movie garb. And a bandana hiding its face since they'd never been identified. But, there had been no cowboy hat; and he'd had the impression of workman's clothes, maybe of ragged blue denim. But, Carson's question was answered as the figure emerged from the steam and looked up.

Mike *wished* there had been a bandana hiding that nightmare face!

Of course he'd seen many horror movies with actors in ghastly makeup. And his father had written bone-chilling descriptions of rotted corpses clawing from graves. But this grisly horror was *real!* Its upturned face was mostly bone with peeling shreds of shriveled skin, no lips to cover its long yellow teeth, no nose to conceal that black cavity, no eyes to fill those empty sockets, and framed by long, dirt-matted hair.

Somehow Mike didn't scream, though he recoiled from the window. Carson made a horrified sound and almost backed into the boiler, but then yelled, "SHIT!" and pulled his gun, aiming at the rotted thing as, leaving its lantern on the ground, ragged garments shedding dirt, it climbed the ladder into the cab.

Mike's eyes flicked to his shotgun, but then to Little Coyote, who was only calmly watching as the decomposing thing appeared. Then, somehow seeing Carson -- in spite of having no eyes -- it threw back its bony remains of a head and a laugh seemed to echo from far away.

Its voice was also strangely distant... which, despite his terror, Mike supposed was logical, since there weren't any lips to form words, no tongue to articulate them, no vocal cords on that spine of a neck, and only shriveled sacks for lungs glimpsed beneath a stark rib cage through tatters of dirt-covered denim. That voice wasn't coming out of this corpse, but out its *grave*... wherever that was.

"Go on shoot, kid," said the thing. "But you're a hundred years too late to drop me with a bullet."

Carson fired anyway, the huge gun bucking in his hands, yellow-orange flame spitting out of its muzzle, the blast deafening in the iron cab... but there was only a puff of dust from the back of the corpse's rotting coat.

It laughed again, and pulled a rusted revolver from somewhere in the remains of its rags and cocked it with a bony thumb.

Somehow, Mike found his voice. "That gun's as dead as you are!"

But a shot blasted out and the cab lamp shattered, spraying glittering shards of glass that clattered off the boiler, leaving only the flickering firebox glow.

"Don't try my patience, boy! My fuse has gotten mighty short waitin' all these years."

Carson and Mike turned to Little Coyote, who simply faced the long-dead thing. "We will do as you say."

"Smart injun," said the corpse, though there was a sneer in its voice. Then it turned to the desert and called, "Come on, boys, an' see what's runnin' trains these days... a injun, a nigger, an' a half-growed kid who don't seem to mind their company."

"Fuck you, bag of bones!" yelled Carson. He almost raised his gun again, but Little Coyote touched his arm. "We have to let this happen."

"Goddamn right you do!" growled another distant voice, as horror multiplying horror, three other rotting, dirt-covered corpses climbed into the ruddy-lit cab.

Maybe Mike was beyond being scared, or maybe numb with terror, but he noted the details of what he was seeing: the other dead things were also dressed -- partly, anyway -- in shreds of blue denim workmen's clothes, circa late 19th century. Instead of cowboy boots, they wore the remains of heavy shoes; and two had ancient miners' helmets with tarnished carbide lamps on their skulls. They were far beyond the wet yellow stench of fleshy decomposition, and their smell was mostly the bronze of dry dirt.

"You're the men who were killed in the cave-in," said Mike.

"Smart nigger," said one of the helmeted corpses.

"Looks like a newspaper... *boy*," said another.

The third laughed hollowly. "Jed, you was always a wit."

Little Coyote said, "You took jobs at the mine so you could plan the robbery."

"...Yeah," said Mike, some of his fear diminishing as his mind began to reason in maybe a spirit-logic way. "You stole a wagon that night and drove it down the rail bed so it wouldn't leave a trail."

Carson's voice quavered a little at first, but strengthened as he spoke: "Then you stopped the train by fakin' the wagon stuck on the tracks."

"And stole the gold," Mike finished.

The first corpse's ghastly head nodded, its smile the rictus of frozen forever. "An' we drove it back on the tracks, an' the sheriff never figured it out."

"We would have," said Little Coyote.

The corpse gave a grudging nod. "I'll give you people that much."

Another rotted thing spoke, "We had to keep workin' at the mine, 'cause it woulda looked suspicious if we'd up an' left."

The fourth corpse's distant voice added, "But we didn't figure the sheriff was gonna keep searchin' so long."

Little Coyote nodded. "Then you died in the cave-in." He smiled. "Which was inconvenient."

"It's our gold!" snarled one of the helmeted things.

Little Coyote smiled again. "You stole it fair and square."

"Goddamn right we did!" growled the other helmeted corpse. "Them mine owners was filthy rich!"

"So, you thought you were entitled."

"Goddamn right we are!"

"But, what did you do with the gold?" asked Mike.

"Yeah," said Carson. "If you got it, how come you're here?"

The first corpse replied, "We knowed we didn't have enough time to get away outta this valley, an' there was gonna be a search, so even if we buried it somebody woulda found it."

Something suddenly clicked in Mike's mind. "You put it in the tender! ...In the water tank! *That's* why it holds less than it should!"

"Right smart nigger," said a helmeted corpse. "The train crew was tied up in the caboose. They could hear us unloadin' the gold, but they thought it was goin' into the wagon."

The other helmeted dead thing added, "We figured after the search was off, we'd unload the gold to a wagon at night when the train stayed over in Coyote Flats, then head for California pretty as you please."

"An' rich as Croesus," another corpse added.

Carson turned to Mike. "But, wouldn't the train people have known the tank didn't hold enough water?"

"They didn't measure the gallons," said Mike. "They just filled it up at the water stops." He faced the first corpse. "You stacked it in the sides of the tank so it couldn't be seen when the cover was open. And the train had come down from Codyville, so the tank would have been about half empty."

The bony figure nodded. "You're almost as smart as a human bein'."

"Too bad you died," said Little Coyote. "You might have gotten away with it."

"We're *gonna* get away with it!" The first corpse jabbed its gun at Mike. "You're a strong-lookin' buck; get your black ass in the tank an' start passin' out them bars!"

"But it's almost full of water," said Carson.

The rotted thing laughed. "Guess I forgot about needin' to breathe. ...Drain the tank an' get to work, boy!"

The safety valve lifted again, gushing a spout of steam at the moon. Carson cried, "We can't let the crown plate go dry! The boiler will explode!"

"Ain't gonna bother us none," said the corpse. "We never wanted to hurt nobody if we didn't have to, but layin' buried a hundred years don't improve your good nature."

Little Coyote asked, "What woke you up?"

The corpse seemed to ponder as the safety valve closed and desert silence settled once more, the boiler pressure rising again. "...Don't right know... 'less it was you startin' up this engine."

"You're buried in that tunnel," said Carson.

"Ironic, don't you think?" Little Coyote said. "Buried so close to what you stole but it's forever out of your reach."

"Not no more!" The corpse leveled its gun at Mike. "Get to work, boy, an' drain the tank!" It tilted its skull to look up at the sky. "They's rules to this, an' there ain't much time."

There must have been some kind of rules, thought Mike; though Little Coyote was right, and living logic didn't apply in the spirit world. Here were four decaying things seemingly material, as were their wagon and horses, yet they must have been ghosts. Were they ghosts condemned by spiritual laws to dwell in their rotting remains?

The other three corpses moved aside so Mike could climb down from the cab. They'd also drawn rusty short-barreled revolvers gripped in skeletal claws; the kind of guns that men like these would have carried concealed. The first corpse waved its weapon at Carson, indicating the tender. "Get on the tank. ...Injun, you get up on the coal to pass them bars when the nigger gets back. ...Boys, you bring up the wagon."

Carson glanced at the pressure gauge, nearing 120 again, as the three other things left the cab after Mike. "But, you're *dead!*" he yelled. "What good is that gold to you?"

"We died for it!" the first corpse snarled. "If we can't have it, nobody can!"

Little Coyote smiled, rising to follow Carson into the tender's coal box. "That is often the way with wealth."

Mike was crouching beside the tender, peering between its two sets of wheels. There was the big drain valve, which would empty the tank in minutes... and the boiler would start to go dry while holding a full head of steam. He turned to gaze across the desert as the trio of rag-clad skeletons started for the wagon. He could see the windmill at his house, where his dad was probably sleeping less than two miles away. What if he made a break for it? Could he get out of this nightmare? ...But, that would be leaving his friends. And, without him to unload the gold, it would take longer while the boiler went dry.

He'd heard what the corpse had said, and Little Coyote's reply. Now he stood up and faced the dead thing. "You died in a mine accident! Maybe doing the first real work you ever did in your lives. It doesn't matter that no one got hurt when you stole the gold; you didn't do anything to earn it!"

The corpse kept its gun aimed at Mike. "Don't gimmie no preachin' 'bout good an' bad, boy! I never believed it when I was alive, an' I sure as hell don't believe it now! ...Drain that tank an' get to work or you won't need to bother with breathin' no more!"

Then, another voice spoke: "I'd say the young man has a good point. ...Drop it an' reach!"

Mike turned to see a man on a horse. Had they ridden out of the desert? Or, had they simply appeared? Both looked very real and alive, the horse glossy brown with saddle and bedroll, the man in typical western gear of boots, canvas trousers and cowboy hat. A silver star on his leather vest glistened in the moonlight as he aimed a Remington .44 at the corpse in the cab... though Mike knew they were spirits because, like Ruff, they seemed to glow. Yet, the man wasn't a movie sheriff who looked like John Wayne or Clint East-wood, but a portly man in his seventies with a bushy white walrus mustache.

"Don't try it, boy!" added the man as the corpse seemed about to raise its gun. The man smiled as Carson, now on the tank, drew his Colt and aimed at the corpse. "Maybe their lead won't damage you... but I guarantee mine will!"

"You're the Codyville sheriff," said Mike, as the corpse's revolver dropped to the ground.

"I'd think that would be obvious," Little Coyote said, arms cros-sed on the tender's rim, chins resting atop them as if he was simply watching a show.

The man tipped his hat to Mike while keeping the corpse in his sights. But then came a trio of raspy clicks as bony thumbs cocked rusty hammers, and the three other things, now crouching in front of the locomotive, leveled their guns at the sheriff.

"You gonna shoot all of us?" asked one. "Them rules work both ways, sheriff."

The sheriff's gun never wavered. "As many as I can, if that's the way you want to play it."

Carson scrambled down on the coal and jammed his Colt to the corpse's skull. "Tell 'em to drop their guns or I'll blow your rotten brains out!"

The skeletal figure laughed. "You ain't even as smart as the injun an' nigger! Just like the sheriff told you, kid, ain't nothin' you packin' can hurt us."

"But *they* will," said Little Coyote, pointing down the tracks.

One of the helmeted skeletons laughed. "That's the oldest..."

But the corpse in the cab seemed to stare, its grisly jaw dropping open, and one of the others turned around. Glowing in the head-light's beam stood a pack of coyotes. There were maybe twenty of them, lips curled back from gleaming fangs; and Mike saw Ruff on point.

"They'll tear you apart," Little Coyote added. "And I don't just mean what's left of you rotting here on earth."

The sheriff smiled at Little Coyote. "'Preciate the posse, son." Then he faced the skeletal things. "Be a smart idea to give up, boys, while you still got souls."

The trio of corpses hesitated, turning to the coyotes. There were low-thunder growls from the pack, and Ruff advanced a few feet. Then, three rusty guns hit the dirt.

"Don't take it hard," said the sheriff. "There's justice where you're goin'."

"We was buried a hundred years!" cried the corpse in the cab. "Layin' there rottin' under the ground! Don't that count for nothin'?"

"Would if you'd learned somethin' there," said the sheriff. "Done a little reflectin' 'bout how you wasted your earthly time. An' a little repentin'. But, don't look like you did." He gestured with his gun. "Into the wagon, boys, we got a long ride ahead."

"Um?" asked Mike, turning to the sheriff as the corpse climbed down to join its crew, the pack of coyotes following as they trudged down the track to the wagon. "Does this mean you can rest now?"

The man looked up at the star-studded sky. "Don't know what happens at the end of that trail, but 'spect I got my own judgment comin'." He faced Little Coyote. "I helped the government steal your land an' run your people out of this valley. Thought I was upholdin' the law; but just 'cause somethin's a law don't always make it right." He turned to Mike again. "Most of us know what's right, son, in our hearts an' souls. The hard thing is to do what's right when it's the hardest thing to do."

"What about the gold?" asked Carson. "What's the right thing to do with that?"

"As much good as you can for others, son. That's what you're gonna be judged by when it comes time to show all your cards." Then the sheriff winked. "But don't forget some good for your-selves."

126

TWENTY TWO

Mike went to the front of the locomotive and stood among the coyotes in the headlight beam, watching as the wagon, one of the dead things driving its team, the sheriff riding behind on his horse, rolled off toward the eastern mountains. The jagged terrain didn't hinder it; and everything soon faded away under the silver moonlight.

Mike turned to Ruff. "Thanks for the heap-big surprise."

Stay on track, said Ruff, and vanished with his companions.

"I heard that!" Carson called from the cab.

"Speaking of which," said Mike. "Little Coyote takes us home."

The safety valve lifted again as if the engine was eager to go. Little Coyote took the engineer's seat as Mike climbed back aboard.

"I *think* I get it," said Carson, climbing onto fireman's seat as Mike took up the shovel. He turned to Little Coyote. "That's why you said we had to stop an' double-act with them ghosts... so we could find out where the gold was."

Little Coyote nodded. "But I didn't expect it to happen that way. Like Mike said, I expected a residual haunting; the ghosts acting out the robbery like it was 1897. And maybe we could have followed them to see what they did with the gold."

"It worked out anyhow," said Mike. "And maybe how it should have."

"'Cause we was there to help," said Carson. He regarded the tender as Mike scooped a shovelful of coal and Little Coyote released the brake. "So, how much is all that gold worth?"

"I'd need a calculator," said Mike.

"Enough to buy our railroad?"

127

"Probably way more than that."

Little Coyote eased out the throttle. There was a hiss and the chuffing began, the locomotive gathering speed. "Which means we're still being tested."

"I guess we always are," said Mike, feeding the firebox.

The engine rumbled along the rails behind the cone of its headlight beam, puffing steam and spouting smoke. The moon had lowered in the west, almost to the mountain tops, silhouetting the iron skeletons of Mike and Little Coyote's windmills.

"Blow the whistle," said Carson as they neared Mike's house. "Give Mike's dad a heap-big surprise!"

Little Coyote did. "Also my sister," he laughed as the haunting cry echoed out.

"An' my mom," said Carson. "...Hey, there she is!"

Mike's eyes widened a little, though -- except for a heap-big surprise -- he wasn't sure what he felt as he saw his father in only jeans, and Carson's mom in a long T-shirt, emerge from the dwel-ling's back door. But, whatever his feelings were, his dad was a man with a life of his own, entitled to choices and happiness.

"Told you my mom is nice," said Carson.

Mike smiled and ruffled Carson's hair in big to little brother fashion. "I'm sure she is, 'cause so are you."

"Hey thanks... everybody wave!"

The boys did as the engine chugged past. Carson's mom and Mike's dad exchanged wondering glances, and after a moment waved back.

Little Coyote's sister, her lush figure wrapped in a blanket, was waiting at the water tank as the locomotive hissed to a halt.

"Heaps?" called Little Coyote.

"Mountains," laughed Dancing Fox.

"Wait till you see the surprise inside."

Mike's dad rolled up in the Rover with Carson's mom beside him.

"Got a cool ghost story for you," called Mike.

"Yeah, they'll have beautiful cubs," said Carson.

"...Huh?" said Mike, turning around. "Who you talking to?"

"The coyote, duh. ...Right *here*, Mike. He's been ridin' with us since them ghosts got busted. ...Ain't he your spirit guide?"

"...No," said Mike, seeing nothing.

Little Coyote smiled at Carson. "But I think he's yours."

THE END

ABOUT THE AUTHOR

Jess Mowry was born in 1960 near Starkville, Mississippi. When he was only a few months old his father took him to live in Oakland, California. Mowry's father was a voracious reader who introduced his son to books at a very early age. Jess attended a public school, but despite his love of reading, dropped out at age thirteen, part way through the eighth grade and worked with his father in the scrap-iron business. In his late teens, Jess moved to Arizona to work as a truck driver and heavy-equipment operator. He also lived and worked in Alaska as an engineer aboard a tugboat and as an aircraft mechanic on Douglas C-47 cargo planes, as well as at a children's refuge in Haiti.

Mowry has written twenty-two books and many short stories about black children and teens in a variety of genres, ranging from inner-city settings to the forests of Haiti, the wilds of Alaska, the Arizona desert, the Caribbean Sea, and the African veldt. While some of his novels are set in Oakland and deal with social issues, such as poverty, violence, drugs, gangs, teenage sexuality, and school drop-outs, Mowry has also written ghost tales, as well as novels featuring Voodoo and African magic, in addition to sea stories, and compiled an anthology of Victorian ghost stories.

Jess Mowry lives in Oakland, California.

THIS BOOK IS ALSO AVAILABLE IN A KINDLE EDITION

OTHER ANUBIS BOOKS

Song For A Summer Night

Mark Dennis

AVAILABLE ON AMAZON